CABO REVENGE

CABO
BOOK 1

ROBERT WISEHART

ROUGH
EDGES
PRESS

Cabo Revenge
Paperback Edition
Copyright © 2025 (As Revised) Robert Wisehart

Rough Edges Press
An Imprint of Wolfpack Publishing
1707 E. Diana Street
Tampa, FL 33610

roughedgespress.com

Paperback ISBN 978-1-68549-665-4
eBook ISBN 978-1-68549-664-7

CABO REVENGE

CHAPTER 1

WE WERE SUPPOSED to meet at a bench not far from where the bridge crossed the river. A lot of homeless congregated under the bridge, sometimes as many as forty or fifty if the weather was bad, so chances were good that nobody would notice us, not at night anyway.

I parked by the pier and started walking the mile or so to the meeting place. I carried a cheap imitation leather briefcase in my left hand, heavy with the weight of a hundred thousand dollars.

It was a cool night, verging on cold. That was fine with me because my black leather jacket hid the Smith & Wesson I carried in a shoulder holster. My little twenty two was tucked away in an ankle holster. I probably overdid it with the firepower, but it's better to have it and not need it that to need it and not have it.

The instructions were simple. The bench was about a hundred yards from the bridge. I was supposed to wait there until I was contacted. I'd turn over the money and Harvey Grant would get his eighteen month old son back.

But nothing is ever as simple as it seems.

I was still a half mile from the bridge when my cell

phone started to vibrate. I'd turned off the ring but the police wanted me to keep the phone turned on in case there was a last-minute change.

"Yeah," I said, feeling vulnerable with both of my hands occupied; the telephone in one and the briefcase in the other.

"Cruickshank, it's Chango."

There was something in Lieutenant Roberto Suarez's voice that I didn't like.

"What's wrong?" I asked.

"Call it off," he said. "We found the boy. He's dead."

I stopped in my tracks. "What happened?"

"Broken neck." Chango Suarez was the father of ten children and I could tell that he was having a hard time with it. "Wherever you are, get out. We know who it is. We'll take him."

I felt pressure building up inside my head as the world whirled around me. I started walking again, faster this time as I bulled through the disorientation I felt.

"Cruickshank! Do you hear me?"

I turned off the phone and slipped it into my jacket pocket. It was as if I was watching myself. I was running now, which was strange because I didn't feel anything, as if my brain wasn't connected to my body.

Following the instructions, when I got to the bench I sat down. After a moment, from somewhere behind me a voice said, "Leave the money and go back the way you came." It was a young man's voice. There was a slight tremor in it. He was enjoying his power but scared at the same time.

I put the briefcase on the ground next to the bench and stood up. Instead of going back the way I came I turned toward the voice. I still felt a strange duality. He was too far back in the darkness to see him. But the other me who was watching knew where he was and what he looked like. He was bald, but it wasn't natural. He shaved his head. He wore a dark blue down vest, a long-sleeved shirt with the sleeves rolled up, faded jeans and work boots.

As I stepped around the bench, I reached inside my jacket and drew the Smith & Wesson.

Surprised at my aggressiveness, he backed off.

"Hey! Whadaya doin'!"

He saw my gun and tried to draw his own. He was so shaken that he fumbled and dropped it before it cleared his vest pocket. I was close enough to see him clearly now. He turned to run and I ran after him. I felt strong and sure, gaining ground with each stride. I wanted to be close enough to make it easy. As we neared the bridge his silhouette was outlined by a fire somebody had going under the bridge. I was just a couple of strides behind him when I raised my gun ....

* * *

I DIDN'T KNOW where I was but I knew it wasn't good. It was dark and I was lying down. I couldn't move. My arms were pinned and there was something tight across my chest. I panicked, cried out and fought against whatever held me. There was a sudden cold feeling on my arm and a little sting and I drifted away.

I was trapped in a strange feverish madness. My only escape was sleep and I slept long and often. The best time was when I was coming out of a deep sleep, but before I was really awake. Then it was as if I'd only dreamed about that night at the bridge, that none of it was real. I knew that if I could hold on to the moment none of it would be real. I fought to hang on, but sooner or later it always slipped away and I knew that it wasn't a dream. I wasn't even sure what "it" was. But I knew that something had happened, something bad.

Finally there came a day when I couldn't go back to sleep, no matter how long I laid there. I reluctantly opened my eyes and blinked against the sudden glare. It took a minute to focus. I was in a bed in what looked like a hospital room, but not quite. There was something different about the little room and its painted cinder block walls. Dina was sitting beside the bed. For the first time I realized that she was holding my hand. She was crying and smiling at the same time. I tried to turn in her direction but I couldn't. I was in restraints.

"How long?" I asked.

My voice was barely a croak. Dina leaned forward.

"How long?"

It came out better that time, a reasonable facsimile of human speech.

"Ten days," she whispered.

"Where am I?"

"You're in the mental hospital," she said.

I felt a jolt of fear run through me as if I'd been hit by lightning.

Dina sensed it, leaned over and kissed me on the forehead.

"You'll be all right," she said. "Everything will be all right now."

* * *

I saw Chango two days later. He was a roly-poly little guy with a thick black mustache and dark hair, the toughest man I've ever known. Now that I was recovering, the restraints were gone and Dina had finally allowed herself to go home for a while. Chango took the chair at the side of the bed that she usually occupied.

"You're a lot of damn trouble," he said. "You scared the hell out of Dina, too."

"It's a gift," I said. "What happened?"

"Dina didn't tell you anything?" he asked.

I shook my head. "Not really."

"I'm not sure how much she knows anyway," he said. "What do you remember?"

I told him what happened up to the time I raised my gun and everything went blank.

Chango got up from the chair, walked to the door and closed it.

"What I say here stays here," he said. "You'll probably tell Dina and I understand that, but nobody else. Got it? Nobody else!"

I nodded.

"The first shot blew the back of his head off. It looks like you fired twice more as he fell. When he was down you stood over him and emptied the Smith, then pulled your twenty two and emptied that, too. By the time you finished, he was a hell of a mess."

"Jesus Christ!" I sank deeper into the pillows, feeling sick to my stomach.

"That's not all," Chango said. "One of the shots you fired as he fell caught a homeless guy in the chest. He lived about ten minutes."

I shut my eyes to stop the tears but it didn't work. They came out of the sides of my eyes and ran down to the pillow.

"You really don't remember?" Chango asked.

"It's called disassociation," I explained. "I've had a problem with it, ever since I was a kid. I thought it was getting better. It *was* getting better."

"The homeless guy was a Vietnam vet," Chango continued. "His name …."

"Stop it!" I said, practically writhing in the bed. "I don't want to know any more."

Chango sat back in the chair and ran his fingers through his hair, waiting for me to settle down.

"The Grant baby started crying and wouldn't stop. The kidnapper lost it, grabbed him by the shoulders, started shaking and broke his neck. I've seen that happen with fucked up parents and babysitters who can't handle it. They never mean to do it. The guy figured he might as well go ahead and collect the money."

There was nothing to say to that.

"We cleaned it up," he said. "Nobody knows for sure what happened out there. If you keep your mouth shut, nobody ever will."

Chango stood up. "Grant's outside. You feel like talking to him?"

"Give me a minute."

As he turned to leave, I said, "Thanks, Chango." He didn't turn back, or acknowledge my gratitude. He just kept going until he was out the door.

State Senator Harvey Grant was a handsome black man with sideburns past his earlobes. Before he got into politics, Grant was a successful criminal lawyer. He planned to run for the U. S. Senate in two years. We've known each other for a while and when somebody kidnapped his little boy he asked me to help.

"How are you doing?" he asked.

"How are *you*?" I asked.

He shrugged. "I'm sure we'll get over it. It's just that right now I don't see how."

He sat in the chair and pulled it closer to the bed.

"They told me what happened," he said. "Or at least everything they thought I needed to know. I know Chango's holding something back, but you couldn't open him up with dynamite."

Grant hesitated and then plunged back into it.

"The thing is, Ethan, don't beat yourself up. You did everything you could. I'm glad that bastard's dead."

"Thanks, Harvey," I said. "But ...."

"There's no 'but' about it," he said.

Grant got to his feet. "By the way, I'm still gonna run. That job we talked about, running security for my campaign, it's still open if you want it."

I didn't have to think about it.

"I appreciate the offer but no thanks," I said. "We're getting out."

"Getting out?" He frowned. "What do you mean?"

"We're going where the past won't kick me in the head every day," I said. "It's not just what happened with your son. It's everything, my whole damn life."

Grant cocked his head to one side as if he wasn't sure what he was hearing.

"So where is this place?"

"Mexico," I said.

CHAPTER 2

I DIDN'T KNOW what to tell him when Big Eddie Heenan said he wanted to see me.

For one thing, I hadn't worked in more than a year and he knew it. I didn't know if I wanted to work anymore, or even if I could.

Getting to Heenan's place wasn't easy either. It involved a two-and-a-half hour flight from the airport in San Jose del Cabo to Los Angeles followed by a two-hour drive north to Oxnard though the always exciting Southern California traffic.

With all this in mind I expressed my reluctance, which included the words "no" and "pain in the ass."

"I've been called that before," he said, ignoring the "no" part. "But trust me, it'll be worth your while. Really."

"How really?" I asked.

"Say at least a hundred and fifty thousand dollars worth of really," he said.

"For what?" I asked.

"For finding a guy."

"That's what you do," I said. "Why don't you find him?"

"There are complications," he said. "Come on up, Ethan. I'll pay your expenses. If it doesn't work for you, all you'll lose is time and since you're probably not doing a goddamn thing down there you've got plenty of that."

He was right, of course. I was rich in time. We'd moved to Mexico for a lot of reasons, most of them having to do with me. For years I'd been fighting my past and mostly losing. We thought that a new life in a new place would fix everything. We'd been going to Cabo San Lucas for years, loved it, and finally decided that was the place. We found a nice house on the beach and moved in. Living is a lot different than visiting and even after a year we were still learning the area and getting comfortable. After selling her public relations business in Thousand Oaks, Dina had come to the conclusion that there was a need for her kind of PR in Southern Baja, mostly specializing in placing stories about the attractions of Baja in American magazines and newspapers. I was a private detective back home, but I didn't want to do that anymore and I didn't see a need for it in Cabo San Lucas anyway. The fact that I didn't look very hard may have had something to do with it, too. Even if I wanted to get back in, I didn't know if I had it in me anymore. It had taken me most of the year just to screw my head back on.

Eddie Heenan was a bounty hunter, or "bail enforcement agent" if you liked it cleaned up. Whatever you called him, he was one of the best. He usually worked out of a bar he owned in a seedy area of Oxnard. Although I knew where he lived, I'd never been to his house. I didn't know anyone who had. He was careful to keep who he was separate from what he did.

"Let me talk to Dina and I'll get back to you," I said.

"When?" he asked.

"Tonight or early tomorrow."

"Don't wait too long," he said.

Dina had left early that afternoon to check out the available office space in Cabo San Lucas. I went out to buy some freshly caught tuna to grill for dinner and it was dark by the time I got back. As I pulled in front of our little house down a dirt road from the highway that connected Cabo San Lucas with San Jose del Cabo, through the window I could see Dina reading in the living room. Brewster, our big black Beauceron who'd adapted quite nicely to life in Mexico, was all over me as I walked into the house, a hundred pounds of eagerness. I bent down and he gave me a slurpy kiss across the face.

Dina put her arms around my neck and gave me a kiss, too.

"I don't know if I like following the dog," she said.

"What can I tell you?" I said. "First come, first served."

I poured a glass of white wine, refilled Dina's glass and joined her in the living room. I sat on the couch and she sat in her favorite wicker chair with her legs curled beneath her. Brewster hopped up on the couch beside me, went around in several tight circles and collapsed with a heavy sigh with his chin on my lap. Both of his people were home and life was good.

I had one of those moments when I realized that everyone that I loved was in this room with me. I experienced a feeling – common in childhood but almost unknown later in life – of a kind of cozy enchantment, the sense of having under the same roof all of the earth's most precious persons and things.

Savoring the moment, I took a sip of my wine.

"Eddie Heenan called today," I said.

"Really." I could practically see Dina's antenna rise out of her dark hair. "What on earth for?"

"He has a job he wants to talk about," I said. "He wants me to come up."

"A job up there?"

"I don't know," I admitted. "I just told you everything I know."

"Are you going?"

"I'm not sure," I said. "Part of me, most of me, I think, doesn't want to. On the other hand, I've got to start working again sometime. If not this, then something else. The question is what?"

Dina took a small sip of her wine. If she put her mind to it, she could make a glass of wine last three hours.

"You don't have to work at all, you know," she said, "especially if I start another business. We did pretty well when we sold my old business. Money's not a problem."

We looked at each other.

"No, you're right, I know better than that," she said, shaking her head.

"It's a nice thought, though," I said. "It's probably dumb for me not to take advantage of it."

"Ethan, this is a chance to do anything you want with your life," she said.

"I know," I admitted. "But I don't know what that that is."

The past year had been perfect. It involved endless walks on the beach and a lot of swimming and snorkeling. I read, I polished my tennis game, I read some more, and I loved Dina. Life was slower and better here. Things that seemed important in our old life didn't matter here. I not only didn't care who won the Super Bowl, I didn't care if there was one. Back in the United States, they were gearing up for another presidential election. I didn't give a damn. The only trouble in paradise was me. I was getting restless.

We talked about it some more when we took Brewster for an after-dinner walk on the beach. Los Cabos is where the Pacific meets the Sea of Cortez at the end of the Baja

Peninsula. Tonight the ocean was a dark brooding mass that was calm and as flat as a frying pan. We let Brewster run free, something we never could have done back home. Some ninny would have pointed out that we were violating one of the thousands of California's can't-do-this laws that wrap people up like a strait jacket and we'd have to ruin the moment and put him on a leash. He dashed up and down the beach trying to catch the tiny sand crabs that always managed to scuttle out of his way. I had no idea what he'd do if he actually caught one. It'd probably scare him to death.

By the time we got back to the house I'd decided that I might as well go. I called Heenan and told him that I'd catch a flight in the morning. I didn't really want to. But it was time to do something. Besides, talking about a job wasn't the same as taking it.

CHAPTER 3

HEENAN'S RED-BRICK driveway ended in a red-brick circle in front of a two-story red-brick house that looked like it belonged somewhere in suburban Chicago instead of on the beach in Southern California. I rang the doorbell and Heenan opened the door. He was dressed in a lime pullover shirt, black shorts that came down to mid-thigh and sandals. Heenan always reminded me of Jimmy Dean's old song "Big John," a guy who "stood six feet six and weighed two forty five, kind of broad at the shoulders and narrow at the hip." He was a local boy who'd played big-time college football before blowing out a knee. After that he was a cop for a while, but had a problem with the rules. What he did now suited him just fine. He got to make most of the rules and the pay was a lot better.

"Let's go out to the deck," he said. "It's too nice to stay inside."

I followed him through the house. It was a man's house, all thick carpet and dark wood, except for one room that appeared to be built around an enormous plasma television on one wall.

"Want a drink?" he asked.

"Beer's good," I said. "It was an ugly drive up from LA, as usual."

Heenan turned left into the kitchen, stopped at the stainless steel refrigerator, reached inside and handed me an Amstel Light. He had a glass of his own in one hand. It looked like it might be scotch on the rocks but I doubted it. Heenan pretended to drink more than he did. It was part of his carefully cultivated image; a hard-drinking muscle head full of bounty hunter braggadocio who sprang to life out of a bad action film. The real man was a lot different, though not many people knew it.

We walked through French doors onto a nicely weathered deck that overlooked the beach. It was high tide and waves pounded the sand and roiled the water practically up to the deck. The marine layer had disappeared and I could see the Channel Islands on the horizon, outlined against the crisp blue sky. We settled into a couple of fake wicker chairs that faced each other across a glass-topped table. "Undaunted Courage," Stephen Ambrose's book about the Lewis and Clark expedition, was on the table. Judging by the dog-eared page, Heenan was about halfway through it.

"Nice place, Eddie," I said.

"It'll do," he agreed. "It will do."

I took a sip of my beer. He took a sip of his whatever. I still didn't know why I was here and it was up to him to tell me. I could hear a chain saw snarling somewhere far away. Even at a distance, it was not the most pleasant of sounds.

"What do you know about Andy Rosa?" he asked.

"Only what everybody knows," I said. "Maybe a little less."

The case was big stuff all over the country. I knew some of the people involved in the investigation and I'd followed it over the internet. What I didn't know Heenan filled in.

Andrew Rosa was kissed on the lips by good luck on the day he was born. One of his ancestors did so well in the oil business that he made following generations of Rosas rich until the end of life as we know it. Unfortunately, by the time Andy came along the family gene pool was a little shallow. Thanks to the trust fund he inherited at age twenty one he was worth at least fifty million dollars. As the years passed, Rosa pared life down to what he did best - sleeping late, working out, fishing, surfing and roaming from one club to another. He was tall and good looking in a dissipated way and possessed a kind of ignorant *savoir faire* that impressed young women who weren't smart or experienced enough to know better.

Rosa's world turned upside down when a junior at the University of California at Santa Barbara claimed that she was a victim of sexual assault at his hands. As she told the story, they met at a popular bar in Santa Barbara. Later that night, he drove her to his house in Montecito where she had a couple more drinks. She woke up the next morning on his couch. She knew that she'd been raped, but had no memory of the specifics. She eventually pieced together what happened: Rosa had put GHB, the date-rape drug, in her drink.

The sheriff's department found all the proof they needed in Rosa's bedroom; a large collection of videos that showed him having sex with a variety of unconscious women while he moved their limbs like marionettes with cut strings. As a bonus, Rosa could be heard making what he apparently thought was fabulously clever commentary. Some of the tapes went as far back as ten years or more. After a long investigation, the police were able to identify a half-dozen of the women, and all of them agreed to testify against him.

Rosa's expensive lawyers persuaded the judge to restrict their client to house arrest and he was fitted with an electronic ankle bracelet. The judge ruled that he could leave his house and travel during certain hours of the day, but only to meet with his attorneys and take care of life's necessities.

For someone of Rosa's wealth, the two million dollar bond was no problem. Bonding is big business, but it's an insurance business. To get started, a bondsman puts up substantial collateral with the insurance company. In turn, the insurance company backs every bond posted through that bondsman for the full amount. Most defendants surrender ten to fifteen percent of the amount the court sets as bail. In Rosa's case, he put up two hundred thousand dollars of his own money to get a two million dollar bond.

The trial had everything, if by everything you mean sex and money. It was one of Court TV's biggest hits. As the trial wound down, things looked bad for Rosa. The testimony was damning, the videos were even worse than the testimony, and Rosa's commentary was worst of all. Good as they were, his lawyers didn't have anything to work with. The usual legal tactic of making the victim look like a slut didn't work because there were too many victims. It didn't help that Rosa never seemed to understand what he did wrong. His smirk alone was enough to make you hope that they'd feed him to the alligators.

One night his ankle bracelet set off the signal that he'd missed his curfew. The police didn't get around to searching the house for six hours. To no one's surprise, they found it empty. Andy Rosa had split. After a recess of two weeks to try and find him, the trial continued without its defendant and he was convicted *in absentia* of one hundred and four criminal counts and sentenced to one hundred and fifty five years in prison.

Rosa jumping bail was Heenan's doorway into the case. It's not generally known, but bounty hunters return almost ninety percent of all bail-jumping fugitives, usually at no cost to anybody but themselves. It's a messy system, and certainly not as glamorous as the movies and television make it out to be, but most of the time it works pretty well.

After the predictable cries of outrage and the usual windy newspaper editorials about lenient judges and sloppy law enforcement, the story had mostly gone away. The police were still looking, but they didn't seem to be any closer to finding Rosa than they were to finding the Abominable Snowman.

And that was everything I knew about Andy Rosa.

"You see, the thing is I have a pretty good idea where the son of a bitch might be," Heenan said.

CHAPTER 4

I TOOK a sip of my beer.

"Eddie, you're going to have to explain that one," I said.

Heenan hiked his knee over the edge of the table and took a sip of his drink. The chainsaw had stopped and I could hear the cry of sea birds circling over the beach. They sounded a lot better than a chainsaw.

"I know Rosa a little, or at least I knew him," he said. "He's an asshole. Always was."

"There seems to be universal agreement on that," I said.

"Since he skipped, I've talked to a few people; his mother, one of his lawyers I knew from before, some friends, a couple of ex-girlfriends, and his housekeeper," Heenan continued. "He's not exactly a Renaissance man. He likes to surf, he likes to fish and he likes to pretend he's the world's greatest lover, except now everybody knows it's bullshit."

I knew where Heenan was going, but I didn't say anything.

"Rosa being Rosa, he'd head for warm weather on a coast somewhere," he continued. "He likes the easy life too much to give it up and he's too dumb to learn anything new."

"That eliminates Switzerland already," I said. "This is easier than I thought."

Like most people, Heenan ignored my keen wit.

"He speaks Spanish, too. At least he always said he could."

"Do I sense a pattern?" I asked. "Does it have something to do with Mexico?"

Heenan nodded. "I'd say the west coast 'cause the fishing and surfing is better there and there's plenty of local and foreign girls."

"The bribing is pretty good, too," I said. "Spread around a little money and half of official Mexico would let him sleep in the spare bedroom. But that still leaves a lot of possibilities. There's Guaymas, Ensenada, La Paz, Mazatlan, Cabo, Puerto Vallarta, Acapulco, and Ixtapa, to name a few, not to mention a bunch of small villages."

Heenan shook his head. "He'd stand out too much in the villages. Besides, Rosa likes the night life. You can't be a swinger if there's no place to swing. His idea of heaven is a place where a lot of drunken teenage girls go."

"Even assuming you're right, that still leaves a lot of territory," I said.

"He's been to Cabo three or four times with those moron pals of his."

"Bingo!" I said. "But why are you telling me?"

"If I find him, I get fifteen percent and a bonus of fifty grand," he said.

I did some fast calculating in my head.

"That's two hundred seventy thousand even without the bonus," I said. "But like I asked before, why are you telling me?"

"'cause you live down there and I can't go to Mexico," he said. "At least I'm not supposed to. I had a problem a few years back chasing another guy. I spent two weeks in a Juarez jail after busting up a couple of Mexican cops who tried to quell me and I had to quell them back. If I go I'll probably wind up in jail again. I'd get out okay, but it might be a while and there's no point in going if I can't do anything."

"So you want me to do it for you."

"Bingo yourself."

He leaned forward, put his big arms on the table, and made his offer.

"Here's the deal: You don't find anything, I pay your expenses. If you find him, or something that leads to him and we get him, I collect and we split the money, including the bonus."

"What makes you think the cops don't know this already?" I asked.

"They probably do, but so what?" he said. "You know how it works. Working through official channels might take years if they get him at all. Even if they find him, like you said Rosa's got a lot of money and bribery is easy down there. Extradition takes a long time. If he runs again, we'd have to start over. The cops might know exactly where he is and still never get him. If we grab him, even if we can't get him out of the country right away there'll be a lot of publicity, too much for even the Mexican government to ignore."

"You really think I'm the one for this?" I asked. "I haven't worked in a while and my last case up here wasn't exactly a success."

"I called you, didn't I?" he said.

I thought it over. It wouldn't be as easy as it sounded. Nothing ever is. But I couldn't find any holes in the idea. It was right in my backyard, too.

"Okay," I said. "I'll do it, or at least I'll try."

"Good," he said. "I'll call my secretary, have her draw up a contract and you can sign it."

"A secretary? A contract? Your pals down at the bar would be appalled."

"Yeah, I know," he laughed. "Don't say anything. I have an image to maintain."

As I got up to leave, Heenan rose and walked me to the door.

"One more thing," he said. "Rosa thinks he's a tough guy. Whether he is or he isn't, by now he might have some people around him who could be trouble. He'll do whatever it takes to stay out of prison. This isn't worth getting killed over."

"Not much is," I agreed.

CHAPTER 5

I GOT in my rental car and checked my cell phone for messages. I was hoping that Dina had called. Instead there was a message from somebody named Roger Boyer who wanted me to call him right away.

I did. After a couple of minutes of being shuffled through protective barriers of receptionists and secretaries, I finally got Boyer.

"I represent a gentleman named Donald Taft," he said. "Mister Taft would appreciate it if you could meet him at his home as soon as possible. It's nearby."

Boyer's voice was so silky it was a pleasure just to listen. It was as if he savored the juices of every syllable and rolled them around in his mouth before turning them loose.

"How did you get this number?" I asked. It was a new telephone service. Nobody had the number but Dina and Heenan and I'd given it to Heenan just a few minutes earlier.

Boyer ignored my question. "If you come, Mister Taft will pay you one thousand dollars. You are under no obligation except to listen to what he has to say."

"You have an unusual way of getting my attention," I

said. "I won't be in town very long. How about right now?"

"That would be perfect." Boyer gave me directions. "I'll tell the guard to let you in."

Taft's house was about forty five minutes away in the rolling hills near Ojai, although calling it a "house" didn't do it justice. It was like saying Buckingham Palace has curb appeal.

The armed guard at the gate let me in after I showed him my driver's license and even then he seemed suspicious. I was surprised that I didn't get frisked and fingerprinted. The driveway was a half-mile long and when I finally arrived at the house it defied description. There used to be a TV series called "The Millionaire." In it, a rich guy named John Beresford Tipton gave a million dollars to some poor slob every week, which usually managed to ruin the slob's life. Tipton's mansion was called Silverstone. Taft's place made Silverstone look like a tract house. It had everything but a moat and a drawbridge.

Boyer met me at the solid oak door, which stood twelve feet high, He was about five ten and a hundred and fifty pounds, with a two hundred dollar hair cut and a gray suit that was either Armani or Brioni. I always got them confused and didn't much care anyway. He looked like the kind of guy who kept in shape by playing squash down at the club, wherever that was, followed by a massage and a weekly manicure.

"I'm glad to meet you, Mister Cruickshank," he said, extending his hand. "I'm Roger Boyer, Mister Taft's counsel."

His voice was even better in person than it was on the telephone. It sounded like poured syrup.

"We appreciate your coming out here on such short notice. If you'll follow me, I'll take you to Mister Taft."

I followed Boyer through the ground floor. I've been on hikes that didn't last as long. We finally emerged onto a large tiled patio that was ringed by a slate wall and overlooked about ten acres of lawn that was so perfectly maintained it could have been used as a putting green. Beyond that was a lake. A finger of piney woods came down to the lake on the other side, with more woods as far as I could see beyond that.

A man was sitting in a padded lounge chair by the slate wall at the edge of the patio and talking on a cell phone. He had dark hair and a neatly trimmed salt and pepper beard. He was casually dressed in deck shoes, khaki pants with a knife-edge crease, and a dark blue long-sleeved shirt with epaulets. Binoculars were on the table next to his chair. He saw us coming, ended the conversation and stood as we approached. We shook hands and he motioned me to a chair next to his.

"Something to drink?" he asked.

"Coffee would be nice if it's available," I said.

I was operating under the assumption that coffee might balance the beer I had at Heenan's place. I was probably wrong, but it was worth a try.

Taft turned to Boyer. "Tell Juanita to bring some coffee, and then see to the check."

Boyer made an efficient little nod and went back into the house, his heels clicking on the tile. It must be good to have a lackey, especially if the lackey was a lawyer. Maybe Boyer wasn't a lackey? Maybe he was a minion? Was it better to have a lackey or a minion?

"I appreciate your coming," Taft said, interrupting my train wreck of thought.

"The invitation was irresistible," I said. "It's the first time anyone's offered to pay for the dubious privilege of talking to me."

"I had to make sure you'd come."

"Mission accomplished."

Taft motioned toward the binoculars on the table.

"When I can I like to work out here and watch the animals around the lake this time of day," he said. "They usually come out of the trees to drink around dusk."

I looked out at the lake.

"There's something out there now," I said. "From this distance, I can't tell what it is."

Taft raised the binoculars to his eyes.

"It's a deer." He handed the binoculars to me. "Beautiful, isn't it?"

The deer stood at the edge of the lake with his front feet in the water, head up and ears alert. It was as if he knew that he was being watched. He was so still he could have been made of stone. Suddenly he bounded into the woods and it was as if he was never there at all.

I returned the binoculars to Taft and he put them on the table.

"What do you know about Andrew Rosa?"

The look on my face must have been priceless. It prompted Taft to ask if anything was wrong.

"You're the second person today to ask me that question," I said.

"What was the reason for the previous inquiry?" he asked.

"It has to do with a case, so I may not be able to tell you," I said. "Why don't you tell me what I'm doing here, then I'll decide if I can tell you about the other?"

"Then you do know about Andrew Rosa?"

I nodded.

"A certain young woman was one of his victims," he said. "She was a senior in college and met Rosa at a club where she and her friends used to go on weekends. You can imagine the rest."

Taft stopped when the coffee appeared along with a

cup and saucer, sugar, several packets of Equal and milk, carried on a silver tray by a Latina dressed in a gray skirt and white blouse. She left it on the table next to the binoculars. I poured myself a cup.

"Afterward, she was angry and humiliated, all the emotions that rape victims often have," he said. "Rosa's trial only made it worse. It was as if everything he did to her was thrown in her face every day. Three days after he escaped, she slashed her wrists and bled to death. Her suicide note explained everything. She wanted to purge herself of it before she died."

It was too dark to see the far side of the lake now. For all I could tell, there might be a herd of buffalo down there.

"It's really quite simple," Taft said. "I want you to get Rosa."

"Mister Taft, I don't hire out to kill people," I said.

"You misunderstand me," he said. "I don't want him killed. I want him to go to prison. I want all the things that can happened to a man in prison to happen to him. I want you to find him and make that happen."

"What is your interest in this?" I asked.

"The young woman was my daughter."

For all the emotion he showed Taft might as well have given me his Social Security number.

"You hide your grief well," I said.

"How I handle grief is none of your business," he said. The words were angry, but the way he said them was not. "The truth is I barely knew her. Her mother and I were divorced when she was very young."

"Then why ...?"

"Because it needs to be done," he said. "When it comes to something like this, traditional law enforcement is slow moving and often virtually incompetent, so I intend to take care of it myself. You are my first choice, but if I don't use you it will be someone else."

Boyer approached from the house, carrying a cell phone.

"Mister Taft, you have a call on the private line," he said.

"I told you we were not to be interrupted," Taft said.

"Sir, it's …" Boyer hesitated. He glanced at me and then looked back at Taft.

"Tell me who it is and stop looking so shifty," Taft snapped.

I recognized the name. Anyone would.

"Tell him I'll call back when I'm free."

Boyer hesitated. "He won't like it."

"I don't care," Taft said. "It'll do him good to hear something other than, 'Yes, sir' from his collection of sycophants. He won an election supported by the ignorant and easily persuaded only because he was thought to be the lesser of two evils. He's not as significant as he thinks he is."

Clearly not convinced, Boyer followed orders and returned to the house.

"That was impressive, unless it was staged," I said. "For all I know, it was somebody trying to sell you a magazine subscription."

"Let me assure you that I don't have to stage anything, for your benefit or anyone else's," Taft said.

Although I wasn't sure that I believed his story, at least not all of it, without mentioning Heenan's name I told Taft that I'd already agreed to do what he wanted only I'd be doing it for someone else. I explained the Mexico theory, too.

"Since we want the same thing, is there any reason why you can't work for both of us?" he asked. "I will pay you very well. Money is not a consideration."

"I don't know," I admitted. "I've never run across anything like this before."

"I also have resources that aren't available to most people," he said. "You will find that my help is worth having."

"Mister Taft, I have no doubt of that," I said. "But you should understand that this could be a wild goose chase. For all we really know, Rosa is living in an igloo at the North Pole."

"Your other client's reasoning seems sound to me," he replied. "By the way, I assume it's Eddie Heenan."

I tried to keep a poker face, although I probably didn't succeed.

"What makes you say that?" I asked.

"I didn't contact you at random," he said. "I know a great deal about you. I know that you see a psychiatrist on a weekly basis, and sometimes more often than that. You were in the same room where your parents were beaten to death when you were five years old and the trauma plagues you today. I know that your wife, Dina, owned a successful public relations agency before your self-indulgent move to Mexico in an effort to hide from your problems. She's very good, by the way. Two of my smaller local companies did business with her, although she didn't know they were my companies. You have no children and one dog, a Beauceron, which is a rare breed in this country, with the quaint name of Brewster. You've worked with Heenan before. Rosa skipped out on a two million dollar bond. The people who are responsible for it want him back. That's what Heenan does and he's very good at it. He's also very good at playing the stock market and other forms of investment, which you prob- ably already know. Quite an interesting portfolio, actu- ally. Like you, he is a man of surprising versatility. I assume he turned to you instead of going after Rosa himself because of some trouble he had in Mexico several years ago."

Since the cat was already wiggling out of the bag, I decided to let it go.

"You're right, Eddie says he can't go back to Mexico," I said.

Taft nodded. He gave the impression that as far as he was concerned it was a done deal, no matter what I thought.

"I'll have Roger see to the details," he said.

"Not so fast," I said. "Before I say yes, I have to make sure Heenan's okay with this."

"What do we have here … ethics?" he asked. "Or are you just showing off?"

I repeated what he said to me earlier, almost word for word.

"Let me assure you that I don't have to show off, especially for your benefit."

Instead of getting angry, Taft only seemed amused. It would take a lot more than that to crack his composure.

"Would you like me to speak to Heenan?" he asked.

"I should be the one to tell him about it," I said. "Once we've talked you're certainly free to contact him yourself."

"When will I hear from you?"

"I'll try to reach him tonight." I said. "Unless it's too late, one of us will call you immediately afterward."

"There's no such thing as too late," he said. "He can reach me at this number."

Taft gave me a business card with only a telephone number on it. There was no name and no address. If it was any more exclusive, there wouldn't be anything on the card at all. I didn't have a card. I hadn't had any new ones made since we moved. It didn't matter. Obviously Taft knew how to reach me.

When I left he was back on the telephone, giving somebody hell.

After the long trek through the house, Boyer handed me an envelope at the door.

"Your check, as promised," he said.

"I'd rather not," I said. "It looks like I'll be working for him anyway."

"Please take it," he said. "Mister Taft keeps his word."

I wasn't sure that I liked the idea, but that didn't stop me from taking the check.

CHAPTER 6

I GOT IN MY CAR, drove to the gate and the guard let me out. After a half mile I pulled off to the side of the road, called Heenan and told him what happened.

"Who the hell is Roger Taft?" he asked.

"I was hoping you knew." I gave him Taft's number. "Chew on it for a while and call me."

I drove to the Marriott where I was staying, parked the car, went to my room and took a long hot shower. Twenty four hours ago, Dina and I were walking on our beach in Mexico, with Brewster happily romping after sand crabs. Things had gotten awfully complicated awfully fast.

After my shower I called Dina. "Kid, things have taken a turn for the weird up here," I said. "This was as strange a day as I've had in a while."

"Boy does that cover a lot of ground," she replied. "I can hardly wait to hear about it."

And so I told her.

"You're right," she said. "It is weird."

"What do you think?" I asked.

"About what?"

"About my taking this case, or cases, or whatever it is."

Dina thought about it. That was one of the things I loved about her. She could be as funny and lighthearted as anyone I've ever known, but she took serious things seriously and gave them her full attention. If I was there with her now I knew that I could practically see the thoughts churning behind her dark eyes.

"I keep coming back to what we talked about yesterday," she said. "Besides, Andy Rosa deserves to go down hard."

"But I don't even know if he's in Cabo," I said. "And if he is I don't know if I can bag him. I'm not sure I have the chops anymore."

"You can bag him," she said. "Tell me about Taft. What's he like?"

"Complicated, mysterious, tough, smart, arrogant, a lot of other things I can't put words to, and probably a lot of things I don't even know, maybe including phony. I'm not sure how much I believe him. By the way, he said that you used to work with two of his companies, only you didn't know they were his companies."

"Really?" I could tell she was intrigued. She'd probably spend most of the night trying to figure it out. "I wonder which ones they were."

"Beats me," I said. "You're the PR whiz."

"Ethan, there's something else," she said. "Daddy's back in the hospital. It's serious. I've got to go."

Dina's father was a retired oil geologist whose career had taken him all over the world. Several years ago, after all his wanderings he retired to Villefranche-de-Conflent, a small walled village deep in the French Pyrenees where he was the happiest man I'd ever seen. Unfortunately his health had deteriorated and he'd been in and out of the hospital several times in the last couple of years. Dina's step-brother Michael lived in Paris and kept tabs on him, but with the news that he was seriously ill there was no doubt that she'd go to him.

"Of course you have to go," I agreed. "I probably won't be worth a damn while I'm working on this thing anyway. You can get a flight out of Cabo to LA or Dallas-Fort Worth, then fly to France from there."

"Actually, I'm already booked DFW to Paris, then south to Perpignon," she said. "I've got a flight out of here tomorrow morning. I'll get a rental car in Perpignon. You understand, don't you?"

"You bet I do," I said, meaning it. "Now I wish I hadn't taken this case so I could go with you."

"Are you going to see your old psychiatrist before you come back home?" she asked.

"You read my mind," I said. "I've got an appointment first thing in the morning."

"I'm glad," she said. "I didn't want to press, but it'd probably be a good idea."

Taft was right about my background. When I was just a little kid, I watched as my parents were beaten to death in their bedroom by two men who'd broken into our house. The cops found me two days later, huddled in a corner and covered with my parents' blood. Although I saw everything, I blocked out what happened that night and it left me with a lot of problems. One of them is that I suffer from disassociation, meaning that sometimes in my head I withdraw from the world around me. Especially when things get tough, sometimes I go blank and enter what the psychiatrists call a fugue state. At other times it's as if someone else takes over and I can't do anything about it. When that happens I don't know what I'm doing, and there have been times that what I did wasn't good. My psychiatrist says that given the right triggers the anger I've built up all these years overwhelms me. One of the risks of disassociation is that you can go away inside your head and never come back. That almost happened that night on the beach last year and it took a long time to recover. I never want to go through that again.

Eventually the psychiatrist would like to find a way for me to break through and remember what happened in my parents' bedroom the night they were killed, but I've never been able to do it. Short of that, he helps me deal with the dissociation, avoid situations where it might happen, although that's not always possible, and fight it off if I feel it coming. Sometimes it works and sometimes it doesn't. When we moved to Mexico, he referred me to another psychiatrist in Cabo, but it takes a while to establish the kind of relationship that makes therapy worthwhile. I thought I'd take the opportunity to see my old shrink as long I was up here.

"How fast do you think this thing will move?" Dina asked.

"I don't know," I said. "There are some things to take care of, but it might go pretty fast. Heenan's got to okay this new deal, too."

"The thing is, I leave early in the morning," she said. "So …."

"… it looks like we won't be seeing each other for a while," I said.

"I'm sorry," she said.

"Don't be," I said. "You've got to go."

"Ethan, is this going to be dangerous?" she asked.

"I doubt it," I said. "Andy Rosa doesn't strike me as the dangerous type. He's just a jerk with too much money."

"But the Mexican police might not like what you're trying to do," she said.

"I hope to win them over with charm," I said. "And if

the deal works out, Taft should be able to help if charm fails."

"You don't know what kind of people Rosa's got around him," she said. "He *is* a wanted man, after all."

"Kid, I don't know that he's got anybody around him," I said. "For all I know, he sits in a twenty dollar a day hotel room, smokes cigarettes and plays games on his computer all day long."

She was quiet for a while, which was not a good sign. I don't think she bought my arguments. On reflection, I didn't think much of them either.

"I love you," she said.

"I love you, too," I said. "I'll call you in a couple of days."

I'd no sooner finished talking to Dina than the phone rang. It was Heenan.

"We worked it out," he said. "It's a better deal for both of us. He's paying all expenses and you get a retainer whether or not you find Rosa. Except for expenses, our deal is the same. You're supposed to see that other guy, the lawyer … "

"Boyer?"

"… tomorrow at ten at his office, if that's okay. Here's the address."

"You have any better sense of who Taft is?" I asked.

"Not a bit," he said. "It's damn strange, too. I did a quick search on him, but there's no record of him anywhere. It's like he doesn't exist, not even that big house of his."

"What do you mean by that?"

"According to the county records, there's nothing there," Heenan explained. "It's part of Los Padres National Forest. Officially, there is no house."

"And all that doesn't bother you? Working for a guy

you don't know anything about doesn't scare you a little?"

"Not particularly," Heenan replied. ""Some of the people I work for, it's knowing what they are that's scary. As long as his check clears I don't care if he fondles sheep and lives in a tree house. We were gonna do this anyway, so Taft getting involved doesn't change anything."

"Even so, it'd be nice to know something about the guy," I said.

"Sometimes knowledge is overrated," he said.

CHAPTER 7

"HOW ARE YOU DOING, ETHAN," he asked. "It's been a while."

It was exactly the way I remembered it. The room was dark, although enough light came in from the closed blinds so that we could see each other. We sat on opposing chairs, although mine was more comfortable, which, I assumed, was on purpose. There was a big aquarium against one wall and the quiet bubbling of the regulator was soothing, no doubt just the effect he wanted.

"It's good to see you again," I said. "A lot's happened in the last few days. I thought we'd better talk."

"Tell me about it."

I told him everything. He didn't interrupt. It took about ten minutes. He asked a few questions about our life in Cabo. I answered them.

"That's very interesting," he said. "I hope you're successful. How do you feel about it?

"Pretty much the same," I said.

"Have you had any episodes since you moved to Mexico?"

I shook my head. "It hasn't exactly been a stressful life down there."

"How did you feel when you were talking to Roger Taft?"

"How do you mean?"

"I'm surprised that you have to ask," he said. "Family issues can be difficult for you. You were talking in an intimate way with a man who lost his daughter. In other words, Taft lost his family, at least part of it. The conversation might have had consequences for you. It might have been painful."

"Believe me, Taft doesn't see it that way," I explained. "He doesn't seem to give a damn about his daughter. I'm not sure what he gives a damn about."

"Ethan, I'm not interested in Taft," he said. "I'm interested in you. It's what you bring to this that matters."

"Anyway, I have my own family," I said.

"Yes, you have Dina," he agreed.

"And Brewster."

"Yes," he smiled. "Brewster, too. But as much as you love them, they aren't a substitute for what you lost at a vulnerable age, not to mention the way you lost it. Certainly this issue is always something for you to be aware of."

We talked for the rest of the hour. It wasn't one of our better sessions. My head was full of the new case and I wasn't able to concentrate the way I liked to. The time that had passed since our last session didn't help. I could tell that he sensed it, too, but he didn't say anything. Some sessions were better than others and we both knew it. Nobody bats a thousand, especially in psychiatry.

"I must confess that I'm not wild about the idea of Dina being away while you do this, although I know it can't be helped," he said. "I wish this was another kind of case, too, something that didn't strike so close to home.

For a variety of reasons, you shouldn't face this alone. This may not be a good time to continue to establish a relationship with another psychiatrist. If you need to talk while you're in Mexico don't hesitate to call me. It would probably be a good idea. Telephone therapy isn't as effective as person to person, but it can still be helpful. It's certainly better than no therapy at all."

"The way you put it makes it sound like dial-a-girl, or something," I said. "Will you talk dirty and everything?"

"Therapy can take some interesting turns, but I wouldn't count on it," he said.

CHAPTER 8

AFTER A THIRTY MINUTE drive south from the Marriott on 101, I walked into Boyer's office at one minute to ten. In my navy blazer, gray slacks, white button-down shirt, red-and-gray tie and black loafers with infinitely sporty tassels, it was all I could do to keep from admiring myself in the mirror.

Boyer's office was on the twenty-fifth floor of a very tall building in Thousand Oaks. I was greeted by a good looking receptionist with dark hair, excellent legs and a voice that sounded like a parakeet on helium. She called Boyer's secretary, told him I was here, rose out of her chair and asked me to follow her, which I did, with pleasure, as long as she didn't talk and ruin the effect.

The office carpet was white and the furnishings were chrome and glass. It seemed so sterile that if I sneezed Boyer would probably have it redecorated. He wore a light gray three-piece suit that looked even more expensive than the suit he wore yesterday. The floor to ceiling window behind his glass-top desk offered a view that stopped somewhere around Fiji. He stood to greet me and we shook hands. He took a seat behind his desk while I slid into a client chair done in chrome and white leather.

"Coffee?" he asked.

"No thanks," I said. "I've had my quota."

Boyer slid a thick envelope across his desk.

"Ten thousand dollars expense money," he explained. "There will be more if or when you need it."

"I'm going to need a hotel room," I said.

"Why?" he asked. "You live there."

"That's why," I explained. "I'm going to act like I'm from up here, or at least from somewhere else. I want Rosa to think that I don't know the turf. The other thing is that I'm going to set myself up as a big fat target and I don't want to do that in my own home."

"I suppose that's fair enough," he admitted. "Where do you want to stay?"

"The Hotel Sol, if I can get in," I said. "It's a good location and I know it pretty well."

"We'll take care if it," he said.

"How do you know there's a room available?" I asked.

"Mister Taft does a great deal of business in many countries and Mexico happens to be one of them," Boyer said. "It won't be a problem."

"I need to make an arrangement about a gun, too," I said.

"I beg your pardon." A frown crossed his face. I couldn't tell if it was a frown of displeasure or surprise. Maybe he was displeased because he was surprised?

"I'm not planning to slather myself in oil and lie on the beach," I explained. "I'll want to be armed and Mexico has some tough gun laws."

"Ah, yes," he said. "To tell you the truth, I hadn't thought of that."

Boyer leaned back in his chair and made a pyramid of

his well-manicured fingers under his chin. I had the feeling it was a pose he used even if he was just ordering lunch. There's nothing like a little sober deliberation to impress a client.

"Would you prefer your own weapon, if you have one, or one acquired in Mexico?" he asked.

"My own, if that's possible."

When we moved to Cabo San Lucas I didn't want to hassle with getting a gun out of this country and into Mexico. Besides, I wasn't sure if I'd ever need a gun again. I left my small collection of firearms in a big safety deposit box at a Ventura bank. I'd picked the Smith & Wesson up on the way to Boyer's office.

"Do you by any chance have the weapon you'll want with you?" he asked.

I stood and unclipped the holster with the gun on my left hip and put it on Boyer's desk. He looked at it as if I'd unleashed a live tarantula.

Without touching it, or even looking at it after the first vaguely horrified glance, he said. "I'll have it delivered shortly after your arrival in Cabo San Lucas, probably at the airport."

"Along with several boxes of shells," I added.

Boyer made a note on a legal pad.

"Based on what you said, I assume that you won't want to use your own vehicle," he said.

I nodded.

"Is Hertz all right? You can pick it up at the airport."

I nodded my satisfaction.

"We should discuss the legal situation, don't you think?" Boyer asked.

I nodded again. I couldn't think of a reason why we shouldn't discuss the legal situation, whatever it was.

"Assuming you find Rosa, and I am not at all sanguine about that because everything about this project seems like pure guess work to me, not to mention something that might wind up doing more harm than good, the logical next question is what to do with him," he said. "The United States and Mexico have certain issues, shall we say, when it comes to extradition. Mexico is usually more than happy to export undesirable aliens, but it does not recognize convictions *in absentia*, life sentences, or capital punishment. The Mexican authorities can be and often are reluctant to hand over people to such justice."

I knew that already, but it didn't hurt to let Boyer talk. Eventually I might even learn something. Boyer obviously enjoyed lecturing and I didn't mind listening while he poured his voice all over me.

"Until a few years ago, bounty hunters such as your friend Heenan and even the more traditional American law enforcement officials would use various legally dubious ruses to drag criminals back across the border while their Mexican counterparts looked the other way," he said. "Until the Kiki Camarena case, both sides were more or less happy with the situation. By any chance, do you remember it?"

I shook my head.

"The name rings a bell, but it's faint," I said.

"Camarena was a DEA agent who was kidnapped, tortured and murdered in Mexico," Boyer continued. "In response, the DEA launched an operation that resulted in the kidnapping of a Mexican national who was suspected in Camarena's murder. He was brought to the United States for trial. The Mexican government demanded that the DEA agent involved in the kidnapping be extradited to stand trial in Mexico. The United States flatly refused. The Mexican government was not happy with that response."

Boyer leaned back in his chair and hiked one leg over the other so that his ankle was resting on his knee. He fiddled with the crease in his trousers, swiveled his chair slightly to the left and gazed out the window. If I had this office, I'd probably look out the window a lot, too.

"Mexico was not the only country alarmed by the DEA's action," he said. "Canada was unhappy with us, too. The assumption was that if such a highhanded venture could happen in Mexico it could happen there, too. Both countries vowed to prosecute any individual who attempted to do what you're about to do on their soil. Currently the official posture is that a bounty hunter must contact the appropriate local officials in Mexico, show a warrant, inform them of the suspect's where-abouts, and then let them make the arrest."

"That's a nice theory, but I doubt that it happens that way very often," I said, knowing perfectly well it didn't.

Boyer turned his chair back in my direction.

"Your doubts are well founded," he agreed. "For one thing, the Mexican judicial system is painfully slow. It can keep a suspect in custody long after his bail has been forfeited in the United States. Even so, if you do manage to arrest – or should I say detain? – Rosa, it would be best to have a Mexican police officer with you when you do. Grabbing him on your own could lead to undesirable consequences."

"It's impossible to know in advance how it might play out," I said. "The circumstances may be, ah, fluid."

I was starting to talk like Boyer and that was posi-tively frightening. I had to get out of here fast.

"Yes, I'm aware of that," he said. "I just thought you might be interested in the lay of the legal landscape, so to speak."

"So to speak," I said.

I decided not to say anything else. I was afraid of what might come out of my mouth.

"Well, I suppose that does it," he said. "You probably have some things to do, so …."

Boyer got to his feet and extended his hand.

"I don't quite know what to say," he admitted. "This is rather unusual for me."

"I don't think it's necessary to say anything, in particular," I said. "You have your job to do and I have mine."

I winked at the receptionist when I left. She did not wink back. Her loss.

CHAPTER 9

TRAFFIC to the LA airport was murder. What could be a ninety-minute drive took three hours. I ditched the rental car and took the shuttle to the international terminal. My luggage was opened, examined and given a seal to indicate that it had been opened and examined. I put my shoes in the little plastic basket, made it though the security check without setting off any alarms, put my shoes back on, found a seat near the boarding ramp and got out my Kindle. I was reading Pete Hamill's novel "Tabloid City," about New York City, a murder, and the slow death of print journalism. It was turning out to be a great book.

I enjoy airports, most of the time. I'm not crazy about standing in long lines, waiting for delayed flights, and listening to babies wail, but I like the sense of possibilities that always seems to lurk just under the surface. Everybody's going somewhere, even if it's only for a long weekend at Aunt Martha's. When I was a kid, flying used to be more exclusive than it is today and I think some of that stayed with me. Add to all that the tingle of anxiety I always feel before I board a plane. Maybe the airline screwed up and assigned six people to my seat? I'm never absolutely sure that I'm on my way until the plane is off the ground.

Boarding for the flight started forty minutes late. Once we were airborne I tried to read but couldn't concentrate. I couldn't sleep either. That was unusual. There have been times when I've been asleep before the plane left the ground. I devoured the snack, drank two beers, and stretched my legs as best I could. I've never found airline food to be that bad, although I've never found it to be that good either. I've always thought that people complain about it to show how sophisticated they are. The food isn't gourmet fare, but so what? It's an airplane, not a restaurant.

The source of my restlessness was easy to figure out. I was about to go to work for the first time in a year and I wasn't sure I had it in me.

It was dusk by the time we landed. Most of southern Baja is desert and looks like it. I always think of Cabo as a mixture of brown earth and bright blue sea. The first sight of it from the air with the Sea of Cortez on one side and the Pacific on the other never disappoints me. We stumbled off the airplane and down the metal stairs that had been wheeled up to the door. The air seemed heavier and richer, and filled the lungs with much less effort.

I walked the fifty yards to the terminal and got in line to have my passport examined, along with the form I filled out on the airplane. I handed my passport and the form to the uniformed guard at the booth. He looked down at the passport, looked up at me, and motioned to another guard standing along the wall. He had an automatic weapon on his shoulder and spoke in heavily accented English, which was a lot better than my limited Spanish.

"Would you please come with me?"

"Is there a problem," I asked.

As this little drama played out, the other passengers in line eyed me as if I'd suddenly turned into a werewolf.

"Not at all," replied the guard, who was so small and looked so young that I wanted to pat him on the head. It didn't help his dignity that his uniform was at least two sizes to big for him. "You must be a VIP."

"Of course," I said, squaring my shoulders and trying to look like a VIP should.

We stepped away from the booth and walked through a door into a bare room a few steps away. A counter ran across the width of the office about halfway in. On the other side of the counter there was another guard and a tall man in a tropical shirt and wrinkled white linen trousers. A cigarette dangled out of the corner of the tall man's mouth.

Nobody said anything, so I did.

"My name's Ethan Cruickshank. What's going on?"

Without taking the cigarette out of his mouth, the guy in the tropical shirt said, "Welcome home, Mister, ah, Cookshrink. My name is Enrique Espada. I work for Mister Taft out of Mexico City. He asked me to help you out."

We shook hands over the counter. The ash on Espada's cigarette was at least an inch long. He took the cigarette out of his mouth and looked at it as if he was surprised to find that he'd been smoking. He dropped it to the floor and ground it out with his foot.

"Do you have your luggage ticket?" he asked.

I nodded. "Uh, huh."

"Why don't you give it to me?" he said. "I'll have your luggage taken care of. It will be placed in your car."

I pulled my airline ticket out of my hip pocket. The luggage tag was stapled to the ticket. By the time I handed it to Espada another cigarette had appeared at the corner of his mouth. He handed the tag to the guard, who left the room from a door on the other side of the counter.

Espada reached down behind the counter and came up with a wooden box about the size of a shoe box.

"Here," he said, "I believe this is yours."

I took the box and slid open the top. It was my Smith & Wesson with three boxes of shells. There was a piece of paper folded in half, too. I unfolded it. The paper was high quality and looked official. There was even a gold seal at the top. But whatever it said, it said it in Spanish, which I still couldn't read very well.

I looked a question at Espada.

"It's a letter from General Miguel Eduardo Urrea," he explained. "It says that you have permission to carry the firearm. If you are challenged, explain that you have a permit from General Urrea and any inquiries should be directed to him. If there are any further questions, show this letter."

"Who is General Urrea?" I asked.

"He is a very influential man, and a good friend of Mister Taft," Espada said. "Here is his number." He handed me a card with Urrea's name and number on it. "It would be best to keep your weapon in the box until you've checked into the hotel. Even with the letter, it's wise not to be too obvious."

I closed the box and put it under my arm. Espada's cigarette already had a long ash on it. He took it out of his mouth, gave it the same surprised look as before, dropped it to the floor and ground it out.

"At that rate, you must smoke ten packs a day," I said.

Espada shrugged. He lifted part of the counter for a pass through, motioned me to follow and then led me out the back door. I realized that I'd cleared immigration. Cool. I could get used to being a VIP.

"Did you really come all the way from Mexico City just help me get through here?" I asked.

Espada shrugged again. "You and your weapon, as Mister Taft requested."

A few more steps and we went through another door that put us outside next to a white Ford Focus from Hertz.

"The key is in the ignition and you'll find your luggage in the trunk," Espada said.

"I bet James Bond never drove a Focus," I said. "I thought they stopped making these things."

Espada already had another cigarette in the corner of his mouth. The ash was about an inch long. I'll never know how he did it.

CHAPTER 10

Located at the tip of the Baja peninsula, Los Cabos consists of San Jose del Cabo, where the airport is, and Cabo San Lucas about a thirty minute drive to the west. Before we moved here Dina and I had been coming off and on for fifteen years.

San Jose is more of a typical Mexican colonial town, with much less in the way of night life and many fewer tourists and good restaurants, although that's changing.

By contrast, downtown Cabo San Lucas is action central, the throbbing heart of the Los Cabos party scene, not that Dina and I cared. Listening to bad music and watching tourists, many of whom had too much to drink, was not our idea of a good time. Most nights we were in bed by nine or ten.

Cabo San Lucas has better beaches, a large marina, a bay, more accessible views and more hotels, a lot more. At night, the funky little downtown teems with activity. A lot of it involves tourists strolling around and buying things they didn't need.

There was a time when tourism fell into three categories: people who were just getting away for a while;

fishermen; and a few surfers. The Sea of Cortez offers some of the best sports fishing in the world. Back in the 1940s and 1950s, long before there was regular airline service or even a commercial airport, a few Hollywood swells often came down in private planes just to go fishing. Now people from all over the world come for the fishing, highlighted by the annual Bisbee tournament in the fall, with its multi-million dollar pot. In recent years golf entered the picture, too. The Robert Trent Jones people built a golf course. So did the Jack Nicklaus and Tom Weiskopf organizations, among others. With its sweeping views and high quality courses, it didn't take long for Los Cabos to become a golf Mecca. Although the place wasn't as cheap as it used to be, it retained most of its old eccentric character. A lot of Cabo was tacky as hell, but for us that only added to the goofball charm of the place. At least the glory of paradise hadn't been drowned with Focus signs and cheap bars. Well, Focus signs anyway.

In short, all kinds of people come to Los Cabos all year around. In Cabo San Lucas especially, somebody like Andy Rosa wouldn't stand out unless he did something to make himself stand out. Heenan's logic was impeccable. This was the kind of place Rosa would love.

The drive from the airport to our house is a knockout. Parts of the highway are high above the ocean and I place it among the most beautiful drives in the world, up there with Big Sur and the Cote d'Azur. But since the sun had gone down I couldn't see it. Except for the scent of the sea in the air, I might as well be driving into Ferndock, Alabama. Fortunately, traffic thins out at night. Americans like to criticize Mexican drivers, but I've never found them to be worse than drivers anywhere else. In fact, they're probably more polite than most. When someone almost runs you down in Mexico, at least they smile at you. In, say, France, for instance, they almost run you down then honk and shake their fist like it was your fault.

Brewster greeted me with his usual gleeful abandon. Dina had only been gone a few hours but he acted like he'd been alone for weeks. After a telephone call to arrange for Josefina, our housekeeper, to take care of him while we were gone, I emptied my suitcase, got a bigger one, and began to fill it up. Brewster hated suitcases. The sight of one always meant that at least one of his people was leaving and he didn't like that one bit. He'd finally gotten over the stage where whenever we got a suitcase out he attacked it. Our theory was that he was trying to frighten it so that it wouldn't accept any clothes, which would make it impossible for us to leave. Virtually every piece of luggage we owned was festooned with his teeth marks, which at least made it easy to recognize on airport luggage carousels.

Back in my car, I slowed down when I came to the outskirts of Cabo San Lucas, thanks to its exciting combination of potholes and speed bumps. With the marina and a gigantic earth-toned hotel, timeshare, and shopping complex, on my left, I turned left from Lazaro Cardenas onto Marina Boulevard and drove through the little town in about two minutes. I took another left, held it for about a quarter of a mile, then turned right and drove up over a steep hill to the Hotel Sol, our hotel of choice until we moved here. It has the best beach, and one of the best views, in the area. The only downside was that the ocean isn't good for swimming. The riptide could probably carry you all the way to South America.

Thanks to the magic of the Taft organization, checking in took about 90 seconds. With the box with my gun in it tucked safely under my arm, I was shown to my room. It resembled an L-shaped studio apartment, with a king bed, a bureau and closet behind two polished wooden doors, a wicker chair, a sofa bed, a bathroom, a kitchenette, and sliding doors that opened onto a balcony that overlooked the pool, with the beach and the ocean beyond that. When I walked out on the balcony in the darkness I could hear the surf pound gently onto the sand, one of the most soothing sounds on earth. It's better than a lullaby.

Unpacking only took a few minutes. Now what? I was hungry, but I didn't feel like going out, especially by myself. I missed Dina. Being here without her didn't feel right. I had to get hold of myself. If I was lonesome already, in forty eight hours I'd be suicidal.

I could either stay in the room and sulk or go eat dinner. Dinner seemed like the wiser choice. I took a shower and put on a pair of cargo pants, a dark blue pullover shirt and sandals and walked down to eat outside at the hotel restaurant, where I treated myself to a lobster dinner and a half bottle of Chablis while I admired the play of the garden lights among the palm trees. Dinner was very good, but it would have been better if Dina was with me.

After dinner, instead of heading back to my room I walked out to the beach. The hotel was quiet, there were only a few people in the palapa bar watching soccer on the overhead television, and the moonlight sparkled on the ocean. I left my sandals by the steps leading from the beach to the pool and walked toward the water, taking pleasure in the cool feeling of sand between my toes. At the water's edge, I stood with my hands in my pockets and looked up at the stars. With no city lights to hide them there seemed to be hundreds, if not thousands, more than I could see anywhere else.

It was one of those bittersweet moments when I missed Dina but there was real pleasure in being here. The yearning I felt made it that much more memorable. After taking it all in for a few minutes I recovered my sandals, trudged up to my room and went to bed.

CHAPTER 11

THE NEXT MORNING I took a photograph of Rosa that Heenan gave me and went to a printer, where I paid to have seven hundred and fifty flyers printed with Rosa's mug shot. The flyers said: "Reward: Five thousand dollars for information leading to the whereabouts of this man - Andrew Rosa. Contact Ethan Cruickshank, Hotel Sol, Cabo San Lucas."

By the time I finished it wasn't even noon and I didn't have anything left to do. The flyers wouldn't be ready until tomorrow. I decided on an early lunch. Or was it a late breakfast? After some deliberation, I concluded that the distinction wasn't important. My meal was followed by a nap, which was followed by a dip in the pool and some quality time at poolside while I read more of "Tabloid City."

After swimming a few laps so I could pretend that I'd worked out, I went back to my room and took a shower. After that I sat on the balcony with a pair of binoculars and watched the fishing boats come in.

Pretty soon it was late enough to start thinking about dinner. Being a man of action, that's exactly what I did. No grass grows under my feet. Planning is everything.

Preparation is my middle name. Ninety minutes later, I ate dinner. After all, if you don't follow up on a plan what good is it? This time I opted for shrimp at a restaurant on the *Playa Medano* on the other side of the *bahia*, where I sat at a table with my feet in the sand and fended off the vendors that always seemed to patrol the beach, selling everything from Mexican blankets and silver to t-shirts and sunglasses. After a year, my command of the language was still limited, but I had "No, gracias" down pretty well as I ate my octopus cocktail and garlic shrimp washed down by two margaritas.

After dinner I drove downtown, found a parking place on an unpaved side street three blocks back from Marina Boulevard, and ambled around, taking my time and going nowhere in particular. I walked up Lazaro Cardenas, down Vicente Guerrero, back up Miguel Hildago, through the Plaza Nautica, east side, west side, and all around the town. It didn't take long. Practically every place I saw promised the best prices in town, no matter what it was selling. I said no to offers for a half-dozen free breakfasts, which also included time share presentations. I was given coupons for free beer or margaritas to what seemed like half the restaurants in Mexico. I refused several offers to go fishing or play golf, most of which also included time share presentations. And I watched the other tourists, who watched me back. None of them resembled Andy Rosa.

Exhausted by another brutal day, I went back to my room, read for a while and went to sleep.

CHAPTER 12

As PROMISED, the flyers were ready the next day. I ran around town like a madman distributing the things. I handed them out to passersby, put them on walls and fences, and left them at all sorts of strategic places. I ran through my batch of seven hundred and fifty in the first forty eight hours and had more printed.

I might have had better luck putting a message in a bottle and throwing it in the Pacific. My telephone did not ring, no one knocked at my door, no one passed me a coded message on a microdot, and no one contacted me to arrange a midnight meeting under a street light wearing a trench coat and fedora.

To pass the time I went kayaking in the *Bahia de Cabo San Lucas*, where I was reminded that kayaking is damned hard work. After leaving a handful of the flyers at the booth where I rented the kayak, I went snorkeling a little way up the coast in *Bahia Santa Maria* next to where the old Twin Dolphins hotel used to be, leaving more flyers at the place where I rented the snorkeling equipment. I rented a jet ski and rode it out to Lovers' Beach, where the Sea of Cortez meets the Pacific, leaving flyers where I rented the jet ski. It was a choppy day and I nearly jarred a kidney loose. I strolled through the marina, which was thick with boats, the usual mix of power and sail, handing out flyers as I strolled. There were a handful of live-aboards, but most of them were only here temporarily, although I knew a few people who made a temporary stop in Cabo and wound up staying. I swam, I read, I napped and I regretted not bringing my tennis racquet, even though there was no one at the hotel to play tennis with. I ate at one of our favorite restaurants, Mi Casa, in town across from the square, and decided that it wasn't as good as it used to be. Later, I ate at another favorite, Villa Serena, high over the beach on the highway out of town, not far from our house, and returned to Las Palmas for an encore. I left flyers at every restaurant and gave one to every diner. The response was absolute silence. On the other hand, I was living well on somebody else's money. I was bored silly, too.

At night I prowled the town, handing out flyers everywhere I went. If Rosa was here, it was always possible that I might run into him accidentally. As strategy goes, it wasn't much but for now it was all I had. Unfortunately, the places where he was likely to frequent were places that made me break out in hives.

The clubs were sad, the way they almost always are no matter where they are. None of them would ever be confused with the Stork Club. The topless dancers looked bored and not that attractive, even in the flattering light. The customers looked desperate and a little silly, all of them grimly determined to have a good time. They probably looked at me and thought the same thing. It was an embarrassing thought.

I bounced from the Giggling Marlin, a bar and restaurant where the tradition is to tie up tourists like a marlin and hang them upside down for a photo opportunity, to the Hard Rock Café, which is just like every other Hard

Rock Café, to El Squid Roe, to Mermaids, and on to other places with names I didn't know.

If anything, the famous Cabo Wabo Cantina was worst of all. After a few minutes, I decided that if Rosa spent any time here that might be punishment enough. Dina and I had always ignored Cabo Wabo and now I knew that our decision was a wise one. An over-the-hill, semi-well known rock singer who wasn't much good in his prime, which was sometime before the earth cooled, backed by a collection of musicians with all the blazing talent of a garage band, played loud enough to make my ears bleed while everyone around me cavorted in rapture.

After circulating around Cabo Wabo, distributing my flyers, and talking to three bartenders who said they wouldn't know Andy Rosa from an elk, I gave it up for the night.

Ethan Cruickshank, man about town, was pooped.

I thought about going to the police and informing them of my mission, but decided against it. If they didn't like what I was up to I'd have to worry about Rosa *and* the cops. With all the litter I was putting out, the cops would hear about me pretty soon anyway. The mysterious General Urrea was supposed to be my ace in the hole, but I didn't want to play that card until I had to. For one thing, I didn't know if it would work.

After breakfast on the fifth morning where I discovered that no one had taken any of the flyers I'd left at the restaurant two days earlier I returned to my room and the message light was on. By now I was so bored that the sight of the blinking light practically made me giddy. I called the desk and was told there was an envelope for me. I asked why someone didn't bring it to my room and they replied that they were instructed to hand it to me at the front desk.

I sat on my unmade bed and thought about it. Maybe whoever left it didn't trust the hotel to get it to me? That didn't seem very likely. What did seem likely is that they wanted me to pick it up because they wanted to see who I was, which meant that somebody was in the lobby waiting for me to show up. That way, they would know who I was and I wouldn't know who they were. It seemed like a good idea to turn the tables. I changed clothes and dressed in a white straw hat with a wide brim, a loose tropical shirt, cargo pants and sandals. I wanted to look as harmless as possible, just another gringo doofus out for a good time in Mexico. My gun and webbed holster were clipped to my belt underneath my shirt. I put out the sign that said "Do Not Disturb" on one side and *"No Molestar"* on the other and scotch taped the door to the door jam in two places, one down low and the other up high. I'd done that every day since I got here and the tape was always unbroken when I came back.

I walked to the lobby, but didn't approach the desk. I stood just inside the entrance and scanned everyone inside, trying to etch their faces in my mind. After a few minutes, I walked up to the desk, identified myself, and explained that someone left a message for me.

It was a small manila envelope. I took it, went over to one of the cushioned wicker chairs along the wall, sat down and opened it. Inside was a sheet of eight and a half by eleven paper with a message: "Be at the gazebo in the plaza tomorrow night at 8."

I tilted my head back pensively – or what I thought might pass for pensively – then pretended to reread the message. Instead of reading I was checking out the people in the lobby again. I was wearing sunglasses so no one could see my eyes. Nobody seemed to be paying me any attention, but I expected that. If they were like me, they were working hard at not seeming to pay attention.

I put the message back in the envelope and put it in my hip pocket. I walked out the front of the hotel toward my car in the parking lot about fifty yards away. Even for a short distance, it's not easy to follow someone if they know they're being followed, especially if where you are isn't teeming with people. I was halfway to the parking lot when he came out of the lobby, where I'd seen him browsing through brochures at the activities desk. He was tall and lanky, with long sun-bleached hair tied in a pony tail and a deep tan that told me he was outdoors a lot. He looked like a surfer. Andy Rosa liked to surf. Could it be? Was it possible? Or was I just grasping at straws? Maybe that sun bleached look came out of a bottle? Maybe he was an off-duty life guard? But maybe I was finally on to something.

If he wanted to follow me he'd have to either get in his own car, assuming he had one, or grab one of the taxis parked in front of the hotel. He didn't bother. The last I saw of him in the Focus's rear view mirror, he was standing on the sidewalk in front of the hotel.

Now I had the advantage. I knew what he looked like and he didn't know it. Even better, he thought he had the advantage. It might make him careless, unless I was all wrong and he was just a guy who happened to be standing in a hotel lobby reading brochures at the wrong time. In that case, I would feel like a idiot when I found out. But in the meantime, it felt good to be doing something. I could always feel like an idiot later.

There was only one road leaving the hotel. The road led to a T intersection at the bottom of the steep hill where you could only go left or right. Left took you into town and beyond. Right led to a dead end at an old deserted tuna cannery three blocks away.

I parked to the right about two blocks down. When you're doing a tail, having a nondescript car pays off. It seemed like half the cars in Cabo were rental cars, and they all looked more or less alike. After a few minutes my boy came down the hill, driving a red Volkswagen Jetta. He turned left and I followed.

We slowly drove through town. With all the speed bumps, slowly was the only way to go. It was early enough that there wasn't much traffic. I stayed far enough behind the Jetta so that the driver couldn't see my face in his rear view mirror.

Just outside of town on the coastal highway leading to San Jose del Cabo, he turned right onto a dirt road that headed toward the beach and a series of two story buildings that looked like condos or apartments. There weren't enough of them to be timeshares. After hundred yards he pulled left into a paved driveway. I drove to the end of the road, turned around and parked. I took off my hat and sun glasses, walked around the car and entered the passenger's side, where I had more room to change clothes. I was pleased at the foresight I'd shown by keeping a change of clothes in the car. I might make the private detective hall of fame yet. In case he spotted me, now I had a different look from when he saw me at the hotel. Then I was a guy wearing sunglasses, a white straw hat and tropical shirt and cargo pants. Now I had no hat, no glasses, a white Fila pullover and dark blue shorts. I got out of the car and walked toward the condo, apartment, or whatever it was until I could see the layout through the scrubby bushes along the dirt road.

A closer look revealed that the complex consisted of five stucco buildings. I couldn't see it from where I was, but there was probably a swimming pool in back. It looked like there were four condos in each building. The living room, dining room, kitchen and a bathroom were probably downstairs, with two bedrooms and one or two bathrooms upstairs. The thrust of the architecture was to the rear, with patios on the ground floor and balconies on the second floor. The Jetta was parked in front of an end condo in the second building.

I went back to my car and waited. I was pretty safe. If he came out, there was no reason for the surfer dude to turn in my direction because the road stopped at the beach. From where he lived, it was an easy walk to the beach from his back door. I was sure than when he left he'd go in the other direction.

Two hours later, I was sweating enough to fill the reservoir at the Grand Coulee Dam. I didn't want to start the car and run the air conditioning because that would only call attention to me. Sweating buckets was not terrific, but I had to live with it.

The Jetta came out of the driveway, turned onto the dirt road, and headed for the highway. I let it get out of sight, got out of the car and walked to the condo. There was no name on the door. I pressed the buzzer. No one answered. It was the same with the other three condos in the building. I couldn't tell if they were empty because no one lived there or because there was nobody home. Either way, it made my job easier. I walked around back, confirmed there was a pool, a big one, too, and peered through the glass sliding door of the condo. It was furnished in standard upscale Mexican, similar to my hotel room; simple but functional, with blue tiled floors, stucco walls and Mexican primitive furniture. The layout appeared to be what I suspected.

My nosing around was interrupted when a young couple came walking up from the beach hand in hand. Caught like the Peeping Tom I was, I decided to brazen it out and walked toward them like I had nothing to worry about.

We met by the big rectangular pool. They were in their early twenties. I was betting honeymoon. They weren't exactly the best looking couple I'd ever seen. His brown hair was cut in a mullet and his wet baggy shorts rode low on his skinny hips. She had three tattoos that I could see and needed to lose about twenty-five pounds if she wanted to do justice to her bikini. I've seen eye patches with more material. Still, they were obviously happy with each other. More power to them, I thought. Ugly people need love, too. As they got closer, he stepped out in front to protect his sweetie in case I was a bad guy. I gave him points for that, but not enough to cancel the mullet.

"I'm glad you two came along," I said. "Tell me, are these places rentals?"

"I can't say about all of 'em, but ours is," he replied.

"It's just that I come down here every year from Seattle and this sure is a handy location," I explained. "It's close enough to town to be convenient but far enough away for peace and quiet. It beats the heck out of a hotel room. You don't know who I can contact about renting one, do you?"

"Tell you what," said the mullet, who'd relaxed now that he knew I didn't want to ravish his sweetie. "If you'll wait a minute, we can give you the address where we picked up the key. We have the guy's name, too."

"That'd be swell," I said.

That was a nice touch. I was proud of myself. You can always trust a man who says "swell."

"I'll get it, Larry," she volunteered, turning toward their condo one building down from the one I was investigating.

"While you're there could you get me a beer, honey," he asked.

She cheerily waved her hand in reply.

"Would you like one, Mister?" he asked.

"I appreciate it, but no thanks," I said.

I was rolling now, inventing like a champ.

"I'm afraid I had a few too many last night," I admitted, motioning to my soaked shirt. "Looks like I'm sweating it out today, too. You guys come down here often?"

"We're on our honeymoon," he said proudly. "Her Dad rented this place for us. We're from Fresno."

Ethan Cruickshank, psychic. I must remember to use this power only for good.

We waited in silence. I thought that I'd covered myself pretty well. If he happened to talk to the surfer dude I followed all he could say is that some guy from Seattle with a hangover who sweat like a horse asked about renting one of these places because he came down here a lot and liked the location. Not only that, he said "swell." What could be more innocent?

Honey returned with two cans of Budweiser, one for him and one for her, along with a name and address scribbled on a piece of paper torn from a yellow legal pad. The name was Jesus Hernandez. The address was downtown at the corner of Lazaro Cardenas and Ignacio Zaragoza. I noticed that instead of dotting her Is she drew little hearts over them. Yuck.

"Here you go," she said. "Hope it helps."

I said thanks and added my congratulations.

"I hope you two are always as happy as you look right now," I said. "It's nice to see."

Larry put his arm around his bride, gave her a loving squeeze and smiled a proud smile. Honey – I still didn't know if her name was Honey, or he just called her that - raised her hand, waved her fingers and said, "Bye-bye." No flight attendant could have done it better.

I walked back to my car and drove to the hotel. By God, I was that young once. I have the pictures to prove it.

CHAPTER 13

Except for a beer, what I wanted more than anything was a shower. Having both at once might be better than going to heaven.

I parked the Focus in the hotel parking lot and walked to my room. In my eagerness, I had my key out before I saw that the tape on the door was broken. I quietly backed down the stairs. It could be a hotel employee doing something innocent, but that didn't seem likely because the housekeeper always left the door open while she worked. With the Do Not Disturb/*No Molestar* sign hanging on the door knob, the housekeeper wouldn't have come in anyway.

My room was on the second floor in a building with six rooms; three up and three on the ground floor. Identical buildings were scattered all over the hotel grounds, a dozen or more, some taller than others and each of them angled for a view of the ocean. I didn't know who was in my room, or even if they were still there, but if someone *was* there I was willing to bet I could out wait them. There was another way out, but they'd have to jump off the second floor balcony to use it and that didn't seem very likely.

I found a good position underneath the stairs to the second floor and in front of the rooms on the ground floor. From there I could hear the door to my room open and grab whoever it was as they came down the stairs. What if there was more than one? It was standard procedure for someone to be inside and someone to watch from the outside, but that didn't seem to be the case, unless somebody was watching from a long distance. If they were, they weren't close enough to help their pal. I thought about drawing my gun, but I'd have time for that when whoever was in my room opened the door. Hanging around underneath a resort hotel stairway with a drawn gun might be a little gaudy.

Why would someone break into my room? Answer: They wanted to find out who I was and why I was doing what I was doing.

Was there anything in my room that would tell them? Answer: My passport was in the room safe, but it wouldn't take long for a pro to crack it. I didn't know if the person in my room was a pro, but I had to assume they were. Even then, my passport only gave my name, birth date and where I was from. They'd have to run a computer check to find out I was a PI back in the States, although a computer check was easy enough. I brought some files on the Rosa case with me, too. They were on a shelf in the closet behind my shirts. If the files were found, whoever was in there would no doubt interpret it as a clue, although they already knew that I wanted to make contact with Rosa.

But was this related to Rosa? Answer: Of course it was. Coincidence does exist, but I never count on it. Besides, what else did I have to do?

I could hear a song from the 1970s, "Love Will Find a Way," by Pablo Cruise, coming from the speakers at the swimming pool, along with the usual too-loud laughter from the people who had a few drinks at the swim up bar and weren't as hilarious as they thought they were. Thinking about the swim-up bar made my mouth go even drier than it already was. It was better not to think about it, except every time I told myself not to think about it that was all I could think about.

Whoever it was didn't waste any time once they got started. They left a contact message and broke into my room at more or less the same time. Was this dangerous? Maybe. If they were pros they'd probably want to find out who the hell I was before making a move. But what if they weren't? Amateurs are tricky because they're so unpredictable. What if it was the same guy I followed earlier? What if I was checking out his place at the same time he was checking out mine? Weird, but stranger things have happened.

A man and a woman came around the corner of the building and entered the room below mine. He was bald and wore a plaid matching shirt and bathing suit, the kind of fantastically ugly cabana outfit that no one should wear in public, or even in private. She wore a black one-piece suit with a thin cloth something or other wrapped around her waist that concealed her legs to her knees. Judging by the rest of her, hiding her legs was a good idea. Their eyes met mine for a second before they aggressively ignored me. What was I, some kind of pervert who liked to lurk under stairways and ogle badly dressed hotel guests? I didn't blame them. I would have wondered about me if I ran into me under the stairs, too.

When they came out of their room fifteen minutes later they ignored me even harder, but at least they'd changed their clothes. I was getting bored and fidgety. I was also hot, thirsty and starting to offend myself with my own body odor. What the hell were they doing in my room? Calm down, Cruickshank. The problem with thinking of yourself as a pro is that from time to time you have to act like one. Oh, shut up. Aren't you tired of being right all the time? Well, no, not really.

I heard my door open with a soft swish. Whoever it was gently pulled the door shut and came down the stairs. As he moved from the steps to the pressed concrete sidewalk I came up from behind and swept his feet out from under him with my left leg. He hit the ground face first like a sack of rocks. Before he could get up, I had my knee in his back, a fistful of hair in my left hand and my gun pressed against the back of his neck. It wasn't the surfer dude.

"Get up very slowly," I said. If he didn't speak English, we'd be here all day.

Fortunately, he understood. I got off his back, kept a grip on his hair and moved my gun down to his spine just above his waist. I jerked him around and pointed him toward the stairs. He was bleeding from the mouth and nose where his face hit the concrete.

"We're going back upstairs, pardner," I said. "Slowly, one step at a time."

When we got to the door, I let go of his hair, got the key out of my pocket and gave it to him, keeping my gun in his back.

"Open the door," I said.

When he did I gave him a hard shove that sent him sprawling into the room. I kicked the door shut behind me, jerked him upright, pushed him against the wall and started to frisk him with my free hand.

He whirled around with a knife in one fist. He must have had it in his belt and palmed it when I shoved him into the room. I jumped back as he turned and felt a burning sensation across my stomach. I fired twice. Both shots hit him in the chest. I was too close to miss. The gunfire was deafening in the small room. He made an

"Uhhh" sound, fell back and slid down the wall, his fist still clenched around the knife.

My ears rang from the two shots and the suddenness of what happened left me stunned. I looked at my stomach. The knife had sliced through my shirt and left a thin red line across my stomach, not much more than a scratch.

I was still contemplating my navel when all the police in the world burst through the door, breaking it away from its hinges and destroying the lock and the door frame. I tossed my gun on the bed and raised my hands.

"My name is Ethan Cruickshank," I said. "I'm a private investigator. This man broke into my room and tried to kill me."

One of the cops took my gun. Another one yanked my arms behind my back, pushed me down on the bed face first and handcuffed me. There was a lot of talk in Spanish. None too gently, someone grabbed the handcuffs and yanked me to my feet. I looked around for someone who might be in charge.

"Contact General Urrea," I said to no one in particular. "He'll vouch for me."

Everyone in the room froze. It was like looking at a painting. Another uniformed cop entered the room from just outside the door.

"What did you say?" he asked.

"Contact General Miguel Eduardo Urrea," I said. "I have a permit from him to carry the gun. I have his card, too. They're in my hip pocket. If you have any questions, call him."

I hoped that Urrea had as much clout as he thought he did because I had just shot a man and probably killed him. In Mexico you're considered guilty until proven innocent and Mexican jails are not known for their comfortable ambiance or delightful companionship.

I took a good look at the cop who'd asked the question. Judging by the way the others deferred to him, he was in charge. He was one of the handsomest men I'd ever seen. He was about five eleven and gave the impression of slender quickness. His hair and mustache were jet black. He had dazzling white teeth and a kind of dark devil-may-care look that was compelling and dangerous at the same time. He looked like an old-time matinee idol. Put a mask on him and he could play Zorro.

He took the letter and card out of my pocket.

"We will see if what you say is true," he said. "For your sake, I hope it is."

His English was a little too formal to sound natural, but it was only slightly accented.

"In the meantime, would you like a doctor to look at your wound?" he asked.

"Yes, I would," I said. "Thank you."

The wound was superficial, but stalling seemed like a good idea. If they carted me off to jail it might be impossible to talk to anybody.

He jerked his head at one of the other cops, who left the room, presumably to find a doctor.

The handsome cop read the letter. Then he went through my wallet. When he finished, he folded the letter and put it in his chest pocket. Holding Urrea's card in one hand, he punched the numbers into his cell phone with the thumb of his other hand and stepped outside.

The hotel doctor was a balding middle-aged man with a black doctor bag, a short-sleeved white planter's shirt, tan pants and light brown loafers with no socks.

He raised my shirt and examined my stomach.

"This will sting," he said.

He swabbed off my stomach with alcohol. He was right. It did sting, but only a little.

"That's all," he said. "A scratch only. You are lucky."

He fingered my ruined shirt with one hand.

"Your shirt, however, appears to be dead." He nodded at the dead intruder who was still sitting against the wall. "Just like that man."

The handsome cop came back into the room. He said something to one of the other cops who released me from the handcuffs.

"Come with me," he said.

Rubbing my wrists, I followed him outside.

"General Urrea would like to speak to you."

He handed me the cell phone.

"Yes," I said.

"Tell me what happened."

Urrea didn't bother to introduce himself. The voice was deep and thick with authority, a voice that was accustomed to being obeyed.

I told him, but left out the meeting tomorrow night and my tailing the surfer dude. I didn't want company at the meeting. I was afraid Urrea might send some uniforms and scare off whoever might show up.

"I see," he said when I finished. "I assume that you're not telling me everything. In your place, I would not, although that might be rather dangerous for you. Return the telephone to the officer."

They talked briefly. Rather, Urrea talked and the handsome cop listened.

He handed me the telephone again.

"I have taken care of the situation," Urrea said. "You will not be taken into custody. You will retain your firearm and you are free to go about your business."

"Thank you," I said.

"I advise you to rely on Lieutenant Valencia. If you see fit, take him into your confidence. He is a most capable man. I have had my eye on him for some time. You would do well to make him your ally."

The line went dead. I returned the cell phone to Valencia, who gave me Urrea's letter and card in return.

"Not much on the social niceties, is he?" I said.

"With General Urrea, the social niceties are not necessary," he said.

"He said you're a good man."

"He said the same about you."

"How would he know?" I asked.

"The General knows what he needs to know," he said.

It took almost an hour to sort everything out. Some medical types came, zipped the guy I'd killed in a black body bag, put him on a little trolley, worked him out the door and carried him down the stairs. At the bottom of the stairs they lowered the wheels and took him away. Two hotel workers showed up with wood for a new door jam and a new door. It only took about ten minutes to make the repair. By the time everybody was finished, it was as if it never happened.

I was alone with Valencia. I assumed that it was no accident.

"I have a few things that I wish to say. General Urrea said that I should leave you to continue on your assignment and even cooperate if necessary. He told me what that assignment is. While I agree that this Rosa is a pig, you don't even know if he's here. It's possible that this didn't have anything to do with the man you're looking for. This might have been just another hotel break in. Or perhaps he saw one of your flyers and wanted to see if you were foolish enough to keep the five thousand dollars in your room? Whatever the motive, I am not comfortable with you operating without concern for Mexican law or custom. You people have ridden roughshod over my country for quite long enough. Mexico has its problems, but those problems are for Mexico to solve."

"He did try to kill me,' I protested. "It wasn't my choice. I'd much rather have him alive. I didn't even get a chance to question him."

"I understand that, but I want to you know that you can't play the cowboy in my city," he said. "I will cooperate with General Urrea, but I don't take orders from him. I am a police officer. He is military."

"He seems to have a lot of clout, though," I said.

Valencia shrugged. "But perhaps the extent of that clout could be tested, if necessary."

"Look, Lieutenant, I haven't played cowboy since I was a kid," I said. "I don't intend to start now."

"Good," he said. "Let us hope you keep it that way. I also know that you live here now. You and your wife, Dina, moved to Los Cabos a year or so ago. I am puzzled by why you have taken this room."

"This isn't exactly the kind of work I want to take home with me," I explained.

Valencia rubbed his chin and didn't say anything. His dark eyes never left mine.

"The General asked me to cooperate," he said after a while. "Very well, I will leave you alone for now. But I advise you to be careful."

Before he left, I had to know one thing.

"How did you guys get here so fast?"

He smiled. His teeth were almost dazzlingly white.

"The couple downstairs saw you loitering around underneath the stairs," he said.

"A lot of cops sure responded," I said.

"The man who called was a retired police officer from Boston," he said. "He didn't like the way you looked."

"I wasn't crazy about his outfit either," I said.

CHAPTER 14

WHEN VALENCIA LEFT, I locked the door, angled a chair underneath the doorknob, grabbed a Pacifico out of the refrigerator, put my gun on the toilet tank, took off my clothes and took a shower and drank the Pacifico at the same time. It wasn't very sophisticated, but it felt great.

I toweled off, put on a pair of shorts and a pullover shirt, got another beer and sat out on the balcony where I could watch the swimming pool crowd. Apparently word of what happened had gotten around. I saw several people in and around the pool staring at me while pretending not to.

I was waiting for the reaction that I was sure would come. I'd just killed a man. I told myself the same thing that I told Valencia: He tried to kill me. But it didn't help. I felt empty and sad. I was doing something that until recently I didn't think I wanted to do anymore. I wanted Dina here so much that it hurt. The shrink was right. I shouldn't be doing this alone. What was it Abraham Lincoln said about something that hurt too much to laugh but he was too big to cry? That's how I felt.

The second beer called for several more. They seemed to go down awfully fast. Maybe they weren't making them as big as they used to? They did that with candy bars, so why not beer? The treacherous bastards had to be watched every minute. You can't trust anything anymore, not even candy bars and beer.

Maybe I should call the shrink? I decided to hell with the shrink. I was tired of being so self-absorbed all the time. I was tired of constantly taking my own temperature and sick to death of endless self-analysis.

I opened another beer. The beer led to an inspiration. Dina! That's who I'd call!

"Well, hello there," I said.

"Honey Bun! What a nice surprise! How's it going?"

"Everything's okay," I said. "I've got Josefina watching Brewster while I stay at the Hotel Sol. And Cabo is Cabo, you know, full of sun, sand, surf, et cetera, especially et cetera. It's all over the place."

"I meant the case, you fool. Any progress?"

"A little. I'm sure Rosa's here, or somewhere around here. Right now, that's about all I know."

I was supposed to tell her what happened, how I'd killed a man in my hotel room after he tried to put a knife in my guts, but I wasn't going to, not until it was all over. For one thing, she'd worry about it, and I'd worry about her worrying about it. With her father's health, she had enough to worry about. She'd get mad at me later when she found out, but she'd get over it. She'd even understand, eventually. I couldn't remember a time when I got in trouble keeping my big mouth shut.

"Ethan, is anything wrong?" she asked. "There's something in your voice."

When you've been married as long as we have you can tell. Fortunately, I was ready for it.

"To tell you the truth, I may have had one or two more beers than is recommended for a balanced diet," I said. "If I stand up, I might fall off the balcony."

She laughed. "Sounds like a tough case."

"It is, but only because I miss you."

We talked for a while longer. I just needed to hear the sound of her voice.

"How's your Dad?"

"He's supposed to get out of the hospital tomorrow," she said. "The problem is that every time he goes in he stays a little longer and he's a little weaker. You know what that means."

"Yeah," I said. "I'm sorry. Tell him I love his daughter."

"I love you, too, H. Bun."

I didn't know if I felt better or worse for having talked to her. Before I could get too morose and hang myself with a towel, I called Valencia.

"Lieutenant, it's Ethan Cruickshank," I said. "I'm sorry to bother you."

"I doubt it," he said. "What do you want?"

"Do you know a man named Jesus Hernandez?" I asked. I gave him the address the love birds had given me. "He's in real estate."

"Yes, I know him, or of him," he said. "He's been in Los Cabos forever. He buys properties, refurbishes them if necessary, holds them long enough to make a nice profit, and sells them."

"Is he legitimate?" I asked.

"As far as I know," he said.

"Thank you," I said.

"What does this has to do with what you are working on?" he asked.

I didn't say anything.

"Yes, of course," he said. "Well, at least try not to shoot anyone else for the rest of the day."

"My plan exactly," I said.

"You're starting to get on my nerves," he said.

"I have that effect in my country, too," I said.

My head felt fuzzy from the beer. I put on my bathing suit, went down to the pool and swam laps. The pool was crowded with men who'd been out fishing all day. Now they were cooling off in the pool, pouring down the alcohol, and regaling each other with their adventures on the high seas. Eat your heart out, Ernest Hemingway. With my brand new reputation as the hotel's resident shootist, I noticed that they cleared a path for me as I swam. There's an upside to everything.

I swam enough to work off the alcohol, toweled myself dry, flopped down in a lounge chair and read my book. I ought to be out detecting, but the day's events had taken a lot out of me and it would take a while to get it back.

How was your day? Well, I ate breakfast and got a message to meet somebody tomorrow night who might or might not help me find Rosa. Then I followed the guy who left the message and sweltered in my car for a couple of hours. After a fascinating conversation with Mullet Boy and Honey I came back to my hotel, discovered someone was in my room, lurked outside and rousted him when he came out. I took him back to my room where he tried to cut out my gizzard before I shot him dead. The police came. I was handcuffed, unhandcuffed, took a shower, drank too much, felt bad, called the love of my life who was with her slowly dying father thousands of miles away, swam in the pool, read my book, and was depressed as hell.

Quite a day. What does it all mean? I didn't know. The pieces would come together later, if they came together at all. That's the way it always seemed to work.

The sun was going down. I took one more dunk in the pool and went back to my room. I changed clothes, walked down the parking lot, cranked up the Focus and went looking for dinner. I wasn't particularly hungry but I didn't have anything else to do.

Now where to find it? Hell, I thought, I'm a private investigator. I should be able to find dinner.

I settled on Mi Casa again, mostly because it's close to where I was supposed to meet who ever left the message tomorrow night. I was familiar with the little plaza but I wanted to scope out the area at night because everything looks different in the dark. I'd check it again tomorrow in the daylight.

Big or small, every Mexican town has a plaza. The size of the plaza depends on the size of the town. This one was a couple of blocks off Marina Boulevard, rectangular with a big wooden gazebo in the center surrounded by an open paved area, which in turn was surrounded by a lot of trees and plants. Although shops and restaurants lined the other side of the streets on both sides, which made up the longer sides of the rectangle, they were mostly closed at night. As the location for a meeting, although it was a public place it was reasonably private, not to mention dimly lit. The possibilities were both good and bad; it was a good place for a meeting, but potentially dangerous, too.

I walked across Avenue Cabo San Lucas to Mi Casa, a funky old restaurant with crude spindled wooden chairs painted in turquoise, red and green. The floor is painted concrete and tile and there are four palapa-covered patio dining levels. I had one of my favorite dishes, *Mole Poblano*, roasted chicken in a dark mole sauce of peppers, seeds, chocolate and spices, and a half liter of unidentifiable white wine because I didn't want any more beer. After a sip of the wine I didn't want it either. The restaurant was crowded and I was the only customer eating by himself, which did nothing to make me feel better. When the strolling mariachi band offered a serenade, I waved them away. There are some depths to which I will not sink.

I drove back to the hotel and crawled into bed. After reading a little, I turned off the light and tried to sleep, but without much success. I was restless and no wonder. I still didn't even know if I wanted to be doing this, but after today I was in too deep to get out.

CHAPTER 15

I WOKE up a little after eight, bleary eyed and grumpy. After two cups of coffee and a shower I called Jesus Hernandez, who said he could see me at ten thirty.

Hernandez's office was a five-minute drive from the hotel. It took me longer to find a parking place then it did to get there. I wound up parking on the next street over. The office was above the *Super Mercado* on the second floor of a two story building with an outside metal stairway. I opened the door expecting to find a secretary or a receptionist. What I found was Jesus Hernandez behind a battered gray metal desk in a tiny cluttered room that looked like he hadn't filed or thrown away anything in fifteen years. There were piles of papers and folders everywhere, including a foot-high stack on the only chair in the room other than the one on which Hernandez was sitting.

He was about fifty. I couldn't tell how tall he was because he was behind the desk, but the parts I could see were remarkably round right down to his pudgy fingers. He looked like Sydney Greenstreet's fatter brother. Starting at just above his ear, a few pathetic strands of dark hair were combed sideways over his head. It wasn't the worst comb over I'd ever seen, but it was close. His round face was so fat that his eyes were slits. His white short-sleeved shirt had food stains on the front and he was puffing away on a five-pound cigar. The room had one door and one window, neither of which was open. With all the cigar smoke, it was like being enshrouded in a vile smelling fog.

He waved me to the chair.

"Please, put those things on the floor," he said.

I did, although I had to move other piles of files and paper aside to make space on the floor.

He offered me a cigar.

"No thanks," I said. "I feel like I'm already smoking yours."

"Do you object?"

"Not as long as I don't have to spend all day in here."

He took the cigar out of his mouth, held it between his first two fingers and stared at it reflectively.

"As you may know, Cuban cigars are legal in Mexico," he said. "My country has its foolish policies, but we are wise enough to know that the only threat Castro has ever posed is to his own people. I still believe that Cubans make cigars better than anyone else, although Nicaragua, among other places, shows much improvement. I smoke fifteen a day."

"It's probably not real good for you," I said.

When he smiled, his fat face didn't crease, it folded.

"Do I look like a man who pays attention to what is good for me?" he asked.

I couldn't think of a polite answer, so I didn't say anything.

Hernandez leaned back in a gray metal chair that matched the desk, except that the chair had green padding on the back, seat and arms.

"So what can I do for you?" he asked. "Are you interested in one of my properties perhaps?"

"Maybe." I described the location and the place. "I want to find out about the sale, if there was a sale, or the tenant if they're renting. If that particular condominium never belonged to you perhaps you can tell me who owns it. Anything you can tell me might help, even if it seems insignificant to you."

Hernandez puffed on his cigar and stared at me for a long time. Just as I was starting to wonder where the smoke went, he released it toward the ceiling with a loud hiss.

"You make an unusual request," he said. "Why do you wish to know?"

When in doubt, tell the truth, at least enough of it to get what you want.

"I'm a private investigator," I explained. "I'm looking for a missing person. I have reason to believe that person may be linked to whoever owns or lives that condo. None of this is a problem for you. No one thinks you've done anything wrong or illegal. I just want information."

Hernandez puffed and stared at me some more.

"And why should I talk to you?" he asked. "How do I know that what you say is the truth?"

"Because it is the truth, because this in no way harms you, because I am willing to breathe the noxious fumes of second-hand smoke from your expensive Cuban cigar, and because General Urrea is interested in this case," I said.

For all his flab, Hernandez was too cool to show surprise, but I thought that I saw his eyes narrow even more than they already were.

"You know the General?" he asked.

"We're old pals," I said. "We went to prep school

together. There's even a theory that we were separated at birth."

Hernandez smiled again. He looked like a Mexican Buddha.

"All right, I made that part up, but he is interested in this case," I said. "Feel free to call him. I'll give you the number. I am also working with Lieutenant Valencia. Perhaps you know him, too?"

"That is sufficient," Hernandez said. "You've established your *bona fides*. I can find out if you're telling the truth with one telephone call and you know it. Therefore, you must be telling the truth."

So far, Urrea's name worked like a charm everywhere I dropped it. If I was ever audited by the IRS I'd mentioned that I was pals with the General. They'd probably give me a medal instead of an audit.

"So what can you tell me?" I asked. "Like I said, even if it seems insignificant to you it might help me."

It didn't take long. Hernandez used to own the condo where the surfer dude lived, along with several others in the development. He sold the one I was interested in, but never met the buyer. In fact, he never met anyone. It was all done through telephone calls, faxes, e-mails and a transfer of money to Hernandez's bank. Where was that old fashioned personal touch when I needed it?

"No one asked to see the property?"

Hernandez shook his head.

"Isn't that unusual?" I asked.

"It is most unusual," he said. "In fact, it was the first time in my experience, although it's possible that someone looked at the property, at least the outside, without telling me."

"But as long as you got paid and there was nothing illegal about it, what does it matter?" I said.

"Exactly."

I thought about my experience with Larry and Honey. If I'd asked, I'm sure they would have shown me the inside of their place. If you seem friendly and harmless enough, people will do that sort of thing. So it was possible that whoever it was saw the property or one like it thanks to one of the residents and set the wheels in motion to buy it without Hernandez knowing that they'd seen it. Still, it was an unusual way to do business. My guess was that the buyer wanted something, wanted it fast, and decided this place would do. Rosa was known to be impulsive, a man who expected instant gratification and always got it.

"Does the name Andrew or Andy Rosa mean anything do you?" I asked.

Hernandez shook his head.

I showed him Rosa's picture. Hernandez shook his head again.

What was the name of the person who bought the property?" I asked.

"As I recall, it was a corporation, not an individual," he said.

"Is a corporate buy versus an individual buy unusual here?" I asked.

"Not at all," he said. "In fact, that's how I do business. There are certain tax advantages here and in other countries around the world, including your own."

"Anonymity advantages, too," I said.

"Yes, that is true," he said.

"What was the name of the corporation?" I asked.

"As I recall, it was Angelo, Inc.," he said.

I felt my stomach flop over as goose bumps rose on my arms.

"Would it be possible to obtain copies of the documents involved in the sale, including the date, time and source of the money transfer?"

"Most of what you ask for is a matter of public record," he said.

"It can take time to obtain public records, especially in Mexico," I said. "If someone with money or influence doesn't want them revealed, they're easily misplaced, too."

"If the information you seek cannot be obtained through the usual channels, that is not my concern," he said.

"Do you have copies of the documents here?" I asked.

He shrugged, which in Mexico usually means "yes."

"May I at least copy the information from the documents?" I asked. "Nothing would leave your office. You can honestly say that you didn't give me a thing."

More thinking and puffing.

"That would be acceptable," he said.

I decided to push him a little.

"You won't let me copy the documents, but you will let me take information from them?" I asked. "That's a very fine line."

"But it is a line," he said. "We all have our standards, don't we?"

Hernandez swiveled his chair and rummaged through some papers that were stacked dangerously high on a credenza along the wall in back of his desk. He passed them across the desk to me. I took out my notebook and pen and began to copy.

I finished about ten minutes later. During that time, Hernandez took two calls, made one, shuffled papers and continued to smoke his cigar until it was no longer than my thumb.

I thanked him for his time and left his office. It was intoxicating to breathe clean air again. My clothes probably smelled like I smoked cigars every day of my life for thirty years.

I walked to my car and drove back to the hotel. I dove into the closet and came up with the Rosa files I'd brought with me. It didn't take long to find what I was looking for. Angelo was the name of the Rosa who made all the family oil money several generations ago. The name of the corporation that bought the condo was Angelo, Inc.

I also noted that before the trial started Rosa plundered his trust fund. He transferred most of it from various accounts in California to Barclay's bank in New York City and from there to a couple of corporations he'd set up in the Cayman Islands. Although he files didn't show it, Heenan was pretty sure that under corporate cover he transferred the money, or most of it, to Switzerland.

I took a shower to get the cigar stench out of my hair, went over my notes and called Roger Boyer.

After being shuffled from the law firm's receptionist with the parakeet voice to Boyer's secretary, I finally got Boyer. I could tell that he had his speaker phone on because it sounded like I was talking into a bucket.

"How are things in Mexico?" he asked.

"Things are very Mexican in Mexico," I said. "Is anybody else in the room with you?"

"Several people," he said. "I was in the middle of an informal meeting."

"Turn off the speaker phone," I said.

"All right," he said.

Boyer sounded a little peevish. He probably didn't like me giving him orders, especially when someone else could hear it. Nevertheless, he did what I told him to do and his voice returned to its normal resonance.

"Is that better?"

"Much," I said. "There's no point in letting anybody else in on this. I need you to do something for me."

I gave him all the information I got from Hernandez. I went over it twice. Before he said anything in reply, Boyer cleared the room. I heard him tell whoever was there to come back in fifteen minutes. Once they left, he asked a couple of questions I couldn't answer.

"Switzerland is difficult," he admitted.

"Yeah, I've heard that," I said.

"But Mister Taft does business there," he said. "That may give us some leverage, although I can't promise anything. At best it will take some time. I'll do what I can and let you know."

"Don't fax or e-mail anything to the hotel," I said. "Call me either at the hotel or on my cell phone. If I'm not here or don't answer I'll get back to you as soon as I can."

"I take it that you're on to something?" he asked.

"It's too soon to say for sure. I'm just looking into some possibilities."

"And you wouldn't tell me anyway, right?"

"That's about it. I don't want to get you excited if it turns out to be nothing."

"At least you're honest," he said.

Next I called Big Eddie Heenan and updated him.

"You've stirred 'em up," he said. "You're making yourself a target, though. Is there anything I can do on this end?"

"I don't think so," I said. "I've got Taft's people working on the kind of financial stuff they have a better shot at than we do. Other than that, I'll just keep plugging away. The important thing is that we know we're on the right track. I was beginning to wonder."

"Okay," he said. "Watch your ass."

"Always do," I said.

CHAPTER 16

I TOOK a taxi from the hotel to downtown Cabo. After cutting through a big outdoor market where I stopped at several booths to fondle the merchandise and make sure I wasn't being followed, I walked to a place that rented motorcycles.

It was time to change my look. I intended to follow whoever showed up for the meeting tonight. In addition to giving me a different look, a motorcycle was more maneuverable. Especially in a cramped downtown like Cabo, that might come in handy.

I drove around town for thirty minutes getting familiar with the Honda Nighthawk I rented. The Nighthawk offered a nice combination of speed and maneuverability. I wasn't ready for a cross-country race, but I didn't have to be. With the helmet, I'd be impossible to recognize, too.

I wanted to check out the meeting location in the daytime. Whatever was supposed to happen tonight it was unlikely that Andy Rosa intended to hand himself over to me. My best guess was that they wanted to find out what I was up to and probably wouldn't move on me with bad intentions until they knew. It was pretty obvious that I wasn't official or I wouldn't be acting the way I was. For all they knew, I might be a writer or a movie producer who was interested in Rosa's story.

But maybe I was wrong? Maybe they wanted to stop me from nosing around and had already decided to kill me? I had to plan for the worst. Anything less was fool-hardy. If I were them I'd want to find out what I wanted, what I knew and, if I wasn't on my own, who I was working for. But I wasn't them. By all accounts, Rosa possessed all the arrogance that comes with inherited wealth and arrogance can be dangerous.

I parked the Honda a block from the plaza and walked over. In the daylight, it seemed a lot more open than it did at night. The plaza was almost twice as long as it was wide. I walked around the periphery, checking where other streets entered into the streets that ran along the plaza's sides. Some kids were playing in that purposeless way that little kids play while their tired looking mothers sat on the benches scattered around the gazebo. A middle-aged Anglo couple sauntered through the square holding hands. The crowd changed when the sun went down. Last night all I saw were Mexican teenagers hanging around because they didn't have anything else to do. Teenagers everywhere never seemed to have anything else to do. You could surround them with all the diversions in the world and they'd complain that there wasn't anything to do. I know I did.

What I wanted tonight was to follow the people who contacted me when they left after I didn't show up. As far as I knew, only the surfer dude knew what I looked like. Therefore, he'd have to be at the meeting. My advantage was that I knew what he looked like and he didn't know it, while I knew that he knew what I looked like.

What else did they know? By now they must know that I'd killed the guy they sent to my room, which meant

I was no pushover. If they wanted to grab me and find out what I was up to, they'd be sure to bring enough manpower to get the job done.

But maybe they didn't know I'd killed the guy? Maybe they thought he lost his nerve or took their money and split without doing the job? Or was Valencia right and the guy in my room didn't have anything to do with Rosa? They'd still have some people around in case I tried something with whoever met me. Of course, I didn't even know if they had "people." All I'd seen so far was one guy.

My guess was that there would be at least three or four of them, with at least one out in the open. If it came to that, he'd give some prearranged signal and they'd move in. Would they try to shoot me? I didn't think so. If this was Mexico City they'd probably riddle me with bullets and I'd be just another body littering the urban landscape. But this was Cabo San Lucas. That kind of thing didn't happen here. Killing a tourist would call a lot of attention to the act. It was bad for business. Assuming that Rosa was behind it, the one thing he didn't want was to draw attention to himself. So I was pretty sure that all they wanted to do was to snatch me, or just talk to me. But pretty sure wasn't good enough.

The bottom line was that it didn't really matter because I had no intention of showing up anyway.

I found a spot on a side street directly across from the gazebo. From there I could see most of the plaza. It would be tougher to see at night, but it looked like the best position I was going to get. It helped that they wouldn't be looking for a guy on a motorcycle. They couldn't see in the dark any better than I could. Even if they had night goggles it wouldn't be much of an advantage. Night goggles are good only if you know where to look.

Satisfied that I'd done everything I could to prepare for the meeting, I rode the motorcycle back toward the hotel. I parked the Honda in the parking lot of El Galeon, a popular restaurant at the bottom of the hill that led to the hotel. I didn't want anybody at the hotel to see me on the Honda. From the parking lot, I huffed and puffed up the hill to my room.

By the time I got there I'd worked up a sweat. I stripped off my clothes, took my third shower of the day, toweled off and climbed under the covers for a nap. I hadn't slept well last night and I was tired. I didn't want to be tired when I went out tonight. There was too much riding on it.

CHAPTER 17

WEARING A BLACK PULLOVER SHIRT, Levis, and black over-the-ankle leather shoes with soft soles, I left the hotel an hour early. The sun was just going down. My Smith & Wesson was in a holster on my right ankle. As a rule, I didn't like ankle holsters, especially with heavy guns. The extra weight made me walk funny, too, kind of like John Wayne. But at least my gun wouldn't dig into my gut when I was on the Honda.

I walked down the hill and turned right at the street below, which took me in the opposite direction from where I'd parked the Nighthawk, and waited to see if I was followed. After five minutes, I decided that I wasn't. I walked to the restaurant parking lot, cranked up the Honda and rode downtown. In a city where parking is at a premium, it's a lot easier to find a parking place for a motorcycle than for a car. For that matter, I didn't even need a parking place. I wheeled the Honda up the slope of a sidewalk in front of a leather goods shop that was closed for the day. The sidewalk was elevated three feet above the side street I'd scoped out earlier. I parked about ten yards back from where the two streets intersected. The elevation wasn't much, but it gave me a little better view. The side street had no streetlights so unless someone got lucky I was as close to invisible as I could get.

A woman showed up ten minutes before meeting time, casually strolling toward the gazebo like she was headed nowhere in particular. I expected the surfer dude but I had to admit that she was a lot more approachable. Her straight dark hair reached to her shoulders. She wore dark sandals, white shorts, and a dark open-necked blouse with no sleeves. Her legs were long and nicely shaped. After several minutes of study, I concluded that her breasts were a little too large for her build. I was willing to bet that they were not nature's handiwork, although nature did a fine job everywhere else. I was also willing to bet that she had a gun in her big leather shoulder bag because it seemed to hang unnaturally heavy from her shoulder. I'm a suspicious bastard.

At eight o'clock she ambled around the gazebo like she was taking in the night, or maybe waiting for a friend, her head slowly turning from side to side as she looked for me. Good. I wanted to work on their nerves a little. After one turn she went back to the steps and stoked up a cigarette.

I left the Nighthawk and edged up until I was not quite at the corner, trying to spot anybody who might have come with her. All I saw were the usual teenagers and two couples cutting through the plaza on the way to Mi Casa. If these people knew what they were doing, there should be someone on both sides of the plaza.

I decided to take a look. I started the Nighthawk and rode down the slope leading from the elevated sidewalk to the side street. I turned left, which put the gazebo over my right shoulder. With my helmet, there was no way I could be recognized. They wouldn't expect me on a motorcycle anyway.

A white SUV had two people in it, both of them men and both of them watching the gazebo. The one on the passenger's side had a cell phone to his ear. I turned right and then right again to the street on the other side of the plaza, where I saw the surfer dude's white Jetta, complete with the surfer dude. He had a cell phone out, too. They probably were talking to each other. I'd found what I was looking for. I went down an extra two blocks, turned right, then right again and returned to my old spot, turning off the Nighthawk's headlight as I coasted in.

By now I was thirty minutes late. There were only a few pedestrians on my side street. I tensed up every time someone passed by, but they moved on and nothing happened. After an hour they gave up. Long legs shook her head in an exaggerated way. It was obviously a signal to the guys who were watching. With long angry strides, she marched to the SUV. She had a nice hip-swaying walk. It was a pleasure to watch.

I already knew where the surfer dude lived. I decided to follow the SUV. If it turned out that they all lived in the same place it would make my job easier. If they didn't, I'd have something else to check out.

When the SUV rumbled past I followed on the Nighthawk, careful to keep some distance between us. That wasn't easy in downtown San Lucas where the blocks are short, the streets are narrow and there's a lot of car and foot traffic. I had to stay close enough so that if the SUV turned and then turned again on a short block I wouldn't lose it. I was glad I was on the Nighthawk. It allowed me to dart in and out of traffic in a way I never could with the Focus. There were enough motorcycles and scooters roaming around so that it didn't seem likely they'd notice mine.

The SUV turned right at the next street and right again toward Marina Boulevard, where it took a left and headed out of town. When it stopped at Cabo San Lucas' only red light I pulled to the right side of the street and slowed to a crawl, moving just enough to keep my balance. When the light changed I gunned the Honda, darting in and out so I wouldn't get caught by the next red light. Once we were on the highway the traffic thinned out and I slowed down to put more distance between us.

I turned off the Honda's headlight so they wouldn't see a motorcycle headlight in the rear view mirror for a long stretch. Several cars coming from the opposite direction flashed their lights to warn me that my light wasn't on. After seven miles the SUV turned right into a common entrance for what looked like several condo and time share projects. I turned on my headlight. There was a guard at the gate. He waved them though, but stopped me. I told him I was headed for Hacienda del Corazon, the name of one of the condo developments I'd seen on a sign out on the highway. If my Spanish was right, it translated as Hacienda of the Heart. With a friendly smile, he waved me through, too. So much for crack security. For all he knew, I was a crazed suicide bomber.

Once I was out of the guard's sight, I turned off the Honda's headlight again. After about a quarter of a mile, the SUV turned left. Another mile or so and it turned right into a big resort on the beach; several multi-story buildings that were probably the typical mix of condos, time shares and hotel rooms. The road leading to the resort rose, then went back down and flattened out all the way to the entrance. I stopped at the peak and watched as the SUV drove up to the pillared entrance. An employee in a white shirt and dark pants opened the SUV doors and my quarry got out. I parked the motorcycle at the side of the road and jogged down. When I looked through the lobby's big glass doors I saw the three of them in a booth in the lobby bar.

The SUV was still out front, waiting for an attendant to take it to the parking garage. I walked into the lobby. It was a risk, but I didn't think it was a big one. None of the trio knew what I looked like. They had a description, but descriptions are tricky. I have dark hair, but a lot of men have dark hair. I'm six two, but a lot of men are over six feet. I'm incredibly good looking and dashing as hell, but I bet that part wasn't in the description. Besides, they weren't looking for me anymore. They'd already tried that and I didn't show up.

I slid into a booth, ordered a gin and tonic and waited. The bar overlooked the resort's swimming pool and the rocky beach beyond. There was a light breeze and the colors of the accent lights looked beautiful on the well-manicured grounds. The bar's windows were open, and I could hear surf in the distance. Unfortunately I was too far away to hear what my trio was talking about. Whatever it was, they said it with feeling. It looked like an argument and I was pretty sure it was about me. There's nothing like dissension in the ranks, especially if I'm the cause.

When they finished their drinks, they left the booth, walked through the lobby and went back outside. The development, which was called Fiesta Mexicana, according to the matchbook cover on the table in my booth, had golf carts that took guests to their rooms. My trio stood outside until a cart pulled up. They climbed in and it chugged away.

I couldn't very well wait for the next one and say, "Follow that golf cart!" Cursing under my breath, I waited until they turned a corner and ran after them. The good news was that once they rounded the corner to a paved path that ran along the side of the lobby building the lighting wasn't very good. Unless they suspected that they were being followed by a huffing and puffing private investigator, then turned and took a good long look to confirm their suspicions, they wouldn't spot me. After about fifty yards, the path turned to the left and ran along the front of the condos/time shares.

The twists and turns in the path kept the cart from going any faster than I could jog, so I managed to stay close enough so that I could see where they got out. It was the sixth building down. The room entrances were all on this side of the building, with balconies on the other side that offered what I'm sure was a sensational view of the ocean. From where I was I could see the doors, but not the room numbers.

They climbed out of the golf cart, tipped the driver and got in the elevator. It stopped on the fifth floor. They got out, turned left and walked about halfway down the length of the building. The two men went into one room and the woman went into the room next to it.

I ran around to the other side. I wanted to see if anybody else was in the rooms with them. On a night like this it would be natural to open the sliding doors and catch the ocean breeze. When I got there the three of them were standing on their balconies, the two guys on one, the woman on another. The building was slightly curved to the outside so that with adjoining rooms they were close enough to talk to each other but couldn't see each other unless they leaned out over the railings. Nobody else came out, which led me to believe that there was nobody else inside. I was sure that neither one of the men was Rosa. I hadn't been able to get a good look in the dim lighting of the lobby bar but they were both too short.

I walked back to the other side of the building. I wanted to make sure that they were through for the night. At two in the morning I decided to hell with it. I was tired and nearly incontinent. I took the elevator to the fifth floor, got their room numbers, walked back to the lobby, peed copiously in the lobby bathroom, walked to the Nighthawk, cranked it up, rode back to the *El Galeon* parking lot and trudged up to the hotel.

All I wanted to do was hit the sack. But after what happened yesterday this was no time to be careless. I turned right just before the hotel's main entrance and walked along a wing of rooms that was part of the original hotel before it was expanded several times over the years. I cut through an open walkway to the beach, turned left, passed through the outdoor bar, which looked kind of sad now that it was closed, and approached the lobby from the rear. I didn't see anybody who looked threatening, mostly because I didn't see anybody at all, just a bored hotel clerk behind the counter leafing through a magazine.

I went back the way I came, only this time I walked down to the beach, where I stopped to see if anybody was staking out my room from the balcony side. Nobody there. I walked past my building on the opposite side from where I'd come if I'd approached the usual way. I stopped at the corner, peeked around. Nothing there either.

Feeling like I'd discovered new and thrilling ways to be paranoid, I went to my room, took off my clothes, put my gun under my pillow, stacked two more pillows on top of that one and fell asleep in about thirty seconds.

CHAPTER 18

IT WAS ONLY seven when I woke up. My eyes felt gummy, my mouth was dry and my head felt like it was stuffed with dirty socks.

I groaned, rolled over and tried to go back to sleep. After a few minutes it was obvious sleep wasn't going to happen. I got out of bed, staggered to the kitchenette, got some coffee going, went into the bathroom and cranked up the shower.

After a hot shower and a shave, I brushed my teeth and drank three cups of coffee. Despite the coffee, what I really wanted was more sleep. I put the Do Not Disturb/*No Molestar* sign out, got the air conditioning going full blast and crawled back into bed. The sheets felt cool and I didn't think I'd have a problem overcoming the caffeine in my system.

I didn't. It was after three by the time I woke up. Even then I stayed in bed, dozing and luxuriating in my laziness. I wanted to push the world away for a while. Even a short time was better than nothing.

It was hunger that finally got me moving. I got out of bed for the second time that day, looked in the mirror and almost scared myself to death. When I went to sleep my hair was still wet from the shower and the result was positively terrifying. It was the worst case of sleep hair I'd ever seen. I looked like a mad scientist.

After another shower to get my hair under control I dressed and practically ran down to the hotel restaurant. It was too late for lunch and too early for dinner, but I threw myself on their mercy and they fed me anyway. I devoured the two rolls in the basket on the table before the waiter turned in my order. After a healthy serving of chili rellenos, rice and beans, four corn tortillas and one large iced tea, I felt almost human.

Now I needed a plan. I had too many people to watch and there was only me to watch them. I needed help. I went back to my room, called the Ventura Police Department and asked for Lieutenant Roberto Suarez.

Besides being the toughest man and best cop I knew, Chango Suarez could have been chief of the Ventura PD years ago but wanted no part of the politics that went with the job. The department owed him about five hundred years of vacation time and I hoped to talk him into taking some of it so that he could come down and give me a hand. Under normal circumstances, he'd probably turn me down. For one thing, the department wouldn't like one of its people freelancing, although irritating the brass wouldn't stop Chango. The problem was that he wasn't the vigilante type. He'd break any rule he pleased, but he had his standards, even if nobody but him knew exactly what they were. My ace in the hole – at least I hoped so - was that Chango's ten children included four daughters. The thought of a predator like Andy Rosa running loose might turn him into a rabid wolverine.

"Suarez," he said.

"Chango, it's Ethan Cruickshank."

"Cruickshank? I thought you'd moved to Mexico," he said.

"I did. I'm calling from Cabo San Lucas. I have a proposition for you."

"Are you telling me you're back in business?" he asked.

"Yeah, I guess so."

"Are you sure that's a good idea?" he asked.

"Your confidence is positively inspiring," I said. "I'm touched."

"Yeah, you are, but probably not in the way you mean," he said, "Okay, propose."

I told him about Heenan and Taft. I told him about everything that happened so far. Then I told him what I had in mind.

"What do you think?" I asked. "We can put Rosa out of circulation and your share of the money would be enough to put a couple of your kids through college."

"Fuck," he said.

"Does that mean yes or no?" I asked.

"It means you're a dumb shit," he said.

"A lot of people agree with you," I said. "But I still don't understand."

"Okay, first thing; the department wouldn't like it, not even a little," he said. "That wouldn't necessarily stop me, but then there's the next thing."

"Which is?"

"Don't you think Rosa's lawyers might have a grand time with the idea of a rogue cop roaring across the border to get involved in the snatching of a guy who didn't even commit a crime in Ventura? Rosa'd probably get off and then sue our asses."

"I see your point, but I'm pretty sure I could keep your name out of it," I said.

"You couldn't," he said. "Sooner or later it'd get out. Besides, there's the another thing."

"What other thing?" I asked.

"In a few days, a week at most, I'm gonna come down on the biggest child pornography ring in Southern California. I've been working on it for three months and I'm gonna bust open those bastards like a piñata. I can't go anywhere right now."

I was disappointed, but he could still help.

"Okay, I understand," I said. "But I still need some help. Got any suggestions?"

"Yeah," he said, "my son."

"Your son?" I repeated brilliantly. "Which son?"

"Antonio, the oldest."

Chango had so many kids I couldn't keep them straight. The only time I'd see them all was at his yearly paella fest. He invited practically everybody he knew to his house and did up big drums of paella in the back yard. Crowds of people would come and go all day long.

"I'm sorry, but I don't remember which one he is," I admitted. "Tell me about him."

"You haven't seen him in a long time. He went to Berkeley on a soccer scholarship. He was all conference for three years. After he graduated he was a cop in San Francisco for a couple of years. He quit to go to law school, but that won't start until fall. He speaks Spanish and English and has a black belt in judo."

"Does he walk on water, too?" I asked.

"If you asked his mother, the answer would be yes," he said.

"Will he come?" I asked.

"That's up to him."

"You trust me with your son?"

"Tony can take care of himself," he said. "He doesn't

need my help. And you know I'd rip your lungs out if anything happened to him."

"Good point," I said. "Where can I reach him?"

He gave me the telephone number.

"Let me call him first so he'll know what's up," he said. "One of us will call you back."

I gave him the hotel number and my room number.

Thirty minutes later, the telephone rang.

"Hello," I said.

"Mister Cruickshank?"

"Yeah."

"I'm Tony Suarez."

"I take it that you talked to your father."

"Yes, I did," he said. "I decided to cut out the middle step and call you myself."

"Got any questions?"

"If you don't mind, I'd appreciate it if you'd go over everything again just to be sure I have it right."

It didn't take as long this time. I was getting better at it.

"All your expenses will be paid and you'll get a daily rate," I explained. "Interested?"

"How much?" he asked.

When I told him, he replied, "Yeah, you bet I'm interested. When do you need me?"

"Right away. Do you have a passport?"

"Sure," he said. "I can fly down first thing in the morning. Is that okay?"

"That'll do fine."

"How do you want me to handle travel arrangements?"

"A guy named Roger Boyer will handle everything. I'll call him and somebody in his office will call you. You'll stay at the Hotel Sol. Once you get in, take a cab to the hotel. We'll worry about getting you a car later. Call me as soon as you get to your room. If I'm not around leave a message and wait for me. Do you have a weapon?"

"Yeah, a couple," he said. "My favorite's a Colt Anaconda."

"A forty four Magnum? This isn't an elephant hunt."

He laughed. "Pop said pretty much the same thing. I like it, though. If you have to shoot somebody, they stay shot."

"Okay, Boyer will arrange to get your weapon into Mexico, too," I said. "Make sure you tell him about it. If there are any problems, call me. If not, I'll see you tomorrow."

"You got it, Mister Cruickshank."

"One more thing," I said. "Stop calling me Mister Cruickshank. I'm not the Green Hornet and you're not Kato."

There was silence on the other end. I could tell something was wrong.

"What's the matter?" I asked.

"I have no idea what you're talking about," he admitted.

"Never mind," I said. "I'll see you tomorrow."

The kid had never heard of the Green Hornet and Kato. The generation gap was never wider.

I called Boyer's office. After the usual shuffling up the line, I told him about hiring young Suarez. I also told him why and gave him Suarez's telephone number.

"You should have checked with me first," Boyer said. "Mister Taft pays me to deal with such things."

I wasn't in the mood to be lawyered.

"You're paid to do what Taft tells you to do," I said. "I can always call him myself. He'll okay it and then he'll wonder why his flunky didn't do his job."

"I am *not* a flunky." I was pleased to hear indignation

in Boyer's voice. I'd gotten to him. The day is not wasted if you've annoyed a lawyer. "That's unfair and you know it."

"You can call yourself anything you want," I said. "Just do what you're supposed to do. I need an extra man. He can come down in the morning."

"All right," he said. "I'll arrange it. By the way, there's nothing yet on the Switzerland situation."

"Do what you can," I said.

Maybe I was a little hard on Boyer, but it didn't bother me. I couldn't think of a reason why it should.

CHAPTER 19

THANKS to my late night and attack of the lazies this morning, the day was shot to hell. I had a lot of people to watch, none of them were Andy Rosa, and I couldn't watch them all anyway. Instead of trying to do the impossible I decided to check out San Jose del Cabo by night.

San Jose didn't have anything like the nightlife Cabo San Lucas offered, which made it unlikely that I'd find Rosa prowling around. But it wouldn't hurt to look.

I'd eaten so late that I knew I wouldn't want dinner. I could always make do with bar munchies. There's nothing like a diet of beer nuts and pretzels to make a man feel like what he's doing is worthwhile.

Most of the action in San Jose was in the hotel zone along the beach. The town itself was a mile or two inland. Except for a few small bars and restaurants, it practically rolled up the sidewalks at night. As I moved from place to place, it was clear that these were not Rosa's people. They were a little too old and a little too quiet. He liked his women younger and his music louder.

I kept looking anyway. I had my usual collection of flyers and gave some to every bartender at every place I went. I explained that he might have a beard or mustache now and asked if they'd seen anyone who looked the guy in the picture, with or without extra facial hair.

My efforts were unsuccessful until the last place, a lounge called *Manana* that was on the third floor of a massive and extraordinarily ugly rust-colored resort that loomed over the golf course next door like it'd been dropped in from another planet.

I slid onto a bar stool and ordered a margarita. I might start to splash if I drank any more beer. Once again it didn't seem like a Rosa crowd. *Manana* was about half full, with a substantial portion of the clientele made up of golfers who'd probably been drinking ever since they stopped chasing their dimpled white balls around. In one corner of the room, two tables were joined together to accommodate seven women in their twenties and thirties who looked like they were well on their way to inebriation, too. Since there was no sign of husbands or boyfriends, I figured that they probably were friends who'd come to Cabo to get some sun and drink their cares away. They appeared to be doing a pretty good job at both.

A woman eased onto the bar stool next to me without bothering to ask if it was taken. Up close she looked about forty, but from a distance she could easily pass for younger, especially with the good dye job that made her blonde hair seem almost natural. She was wearing dark sandals, a loose black skirt with yellow and red flowers on it, and a sleeveless yellow blouse hanging outside the skirt. The dress hiked up to mid-thigh when she sat on the bar stool, but she didn't seem to mind. Her legs were worth showing off and she knew it. The muscle tone in her arms and legs was so good I concluded that she either worked out or swam several times a week.

In short, she was a mature woman who was easy to look at. My favorite. I looked, too, but without seeming to stare. Staring is so tacky. Being a PI has its advantages. You learn to check people out without their knowing it.

Except this time it didn't work. Something in her body language told me that she knew I was looking. Probably part of it was that she was so used to being ogled she assumed that I was ogling her because that's what men did. The fact that I *was* ogling her only proved her right. She turned in my direction and offered the slightest hint of a smile. There was a touch of world weariness there, too, as if she spent too much time in places like this being stared at by men like me. Of course, if she didn't like it, she wouldn't come to places like this. Besides, I wasn't staring that hard.

I leaned toward her so she could hear me.

"Excuse me, but do you come here often?" I said.

She swiveled on the bar stool to face me full on.

"Do you come here often?" she said. "Jesus! Is *that* the best you can do?"

She was more amused than offended. Actually, she didn't seem offended at all.

I laughed. I didn't mean for it to sound the way it sounded.

"God, I hope not," I said. "But the thing is I really want to know if you come here a lot. I'm looking for someone and maybe you can help me. Really. Cross my heart and everything, including scout's honor."

She took a good healthy belt of her drink. It was a dark drink. Probably rum and coke. She was no sipper, one of those people who can make one drink last for a couple of hours. Two or three an hour was more her style.

"Now that's better," she said. "Now it works as a pick-up line and if you're really looking for somebody."

"Number two is tonight's lucky winner," I said. "I feel like I'm in a Cary Grant movie. Is your repartee always this snappy?"

"Repartee? That's pretty good."

"Thanks," I said. "That's nice to hear considering how out of practice I am, even if I'm being mocked."

"Married or gay?" she asked.

"Married," I said.

"How married?"

"Extremely."

"Is she here?"

I shook my head. "Nope. She's visiting her sick father," I said. "We live here."

"Really?" she said. "You like it here?'

"Yeah," I said. "We like it a lot."

"You don't miss life back in the States?" she asked. "You know, football, asshole politicians, too many nosy people, restrictive laws, and all that other crap that makes the USA tick?"

"Someone once said that football represents the two worst aspects of American life; violence and committee meetings," I said. "I'm not interested. As for the politicians, they're everywhere. It's a global epidemic. What about you? What are you doing here?"

She finished the last of her drink. I nodded at her empty glass and raised my eyebrows. She assented without saying anything and I motioned to the bartender for another one. I passed on one for myself. I still had half of my weak but overpriced margarita left. Yummy.

"I live here, too," she said. "I sell real estate. I moved down from LA five years ago.

"What brought you here?" I asked.

"I needed a change after a messy divorce," she said. "We'd been to Cabo a couple of times so I knew I liked it.

I sold real estate in LA, so I moved here, sold time shares for a while and got into real estate, *real* real estate."

"How's business?" I asked.

"I do a lot better than I would back home, that's for sure."

She made a waving motion with her hand in the direction of one of the big windows on the other side of the room that looked out over the golf course, except that it was too dark to see anything.

"I'm in a condo just beyond that. One side looks over the golf course. The other looks out at the ocean. I could never afford to live like that in LA. Even if I could, there's still all that other crap."

"There is that," I agreed. "And plenty of it, too."

Manana was filling up now. The talk and laughter was louder. The canned music was playing the Eagles' "Hotel California." A lot of the music I'd heard since I was on this case was from the seventies. I didn't mind. Some of it brought back memories, songs I hadn't heard in years. Everything seemed to be building to some kind of boozy crescendo that would last for at least a couple of hours. I noticed that the women I'd seen earlier had attracted a more than equal number of men. Maybe sun and booze wasn't everything they'd come here to find. I tipped my glass in their direction. Good hunting, ladies.

"What are you doing here tonight?" I asked.

"I'm meeting a friend in a few minutes," she said. "We're going out to dinner. I thought I'd come early and have a drink. I come in pretty regularly. They know me here."

"Like they used to say on 'Cheers,' a place where everybody knows your name,'" I said.

"Something like that," she agreed.

As she talked, she glanced at her watch to check the time. It was a Rolex, or maybe it was a fake Rolex. You could buy one for fifty bucks on almost any block in Cabo San Lucas. On the other hand, maybe it was real. Maybe business was that good.

I motioned to the bartender for another margarita. I didn't really want another one, but it seemed like the thing to do. I'm always willing to help the Mexican economy, especially on somebody else's money.

"Now tell me, who is this person you're looking for?" she said.

I produced one of the flyers and put it on the bar in front of her.

"Ever seen this man around here?" I asked. "He might have grown a beard or a mustache since this was taken. He might even have shaved his head."

She picked up the flyer and turned it slightly to get better light on it. She stared at it for a long time.

"Yeah," she said. "I have."

I was not ready for that answer and it took a moment to sink in.

"You seem surprised," she said.

"After hearing so many people say no I didn't expect you to say yes," I admitted.

"Why are you looking for him?"

"I can't say, at least not right now," I said. "I can tell you that I'm one of the good guys and you won't be breaking any laws by telling me. There will be no trouble. I'm just looking for information."

I could see the question in her eyes.

"I don't want to prejudice your response," I explained. "He could be public enemy number one or he could be a guy whose rich uncle died and left him ten million dollars and I'm supposed to find him because he doesn't know it. Sometimes people want to help so much they say things they don't really know. Getting wrong information is worse than getting no information at all. It can make for a lot of wasted effort and time."

She thought about that as she swirled the ice in her drink with a swizzle stick.

"Yeah," she said, "I guess that makes sense."

She looked at the picture on the flyer again. This time she stood on her feet and turned so that she could see it in the light from the bar. She handed it back to me and climbed back up on the bar stool, smiling when she saw me glance at her legs again.

"He had a beard, a goatee, actually, and you're right, he'd shaved his head, but I'm sure it was him." She tossed her head to keep her hair from falling across her face. "There's something about his eyes. It's like he's sneering at you, but it's more complicated than that."

I knew what she meant. In every picture of Andy Rosa that I'd seen, he had that same smug look. It was as if he was saying, "I'm richer than you, I'm better than you, and I don't have to live by the same rules." The longer I was on this case the more I wanted to wipe that look off his face.

"He came into the office one day," she said. "Said he was looking for some property; a beach house or a condo on the beach. He said he was from Hawaii, but wanted to buy here because beach property was too expensive in Hawaii and he thought Los Cabos was a better investment anyway. And he's right. It is."

"When was this?" I asked.

"I can't say exactly," she said. "A few months ago."

"Did he fill out a form or anything? Leave any information at all?"

"That's another reason why I remember him," she said. "I have a short form that I ask clients to fill out; name, their current address, the kind of thing they're looking for, price range, how to reach them. Just basic stuff that helps me when I'm looking at property. He wouldn't fill it out. He said he didn't want to commit himself, that he really wasn't prepared to buy; blah, blah, blah. I could tell there was something else going on, but I didn't know what it was."

"How many times did you see him?" I asked.

"Just that once," she said. "He never came back. The whole thing lasted less than twenty minutes."

"Is your office here or in San Lucas?" I asked.

"I've got one in both. I sell all the way up the coast to La Paz. He came to the one in San Lucas. It's in a little L-shaped strip mall just outside of town. There's a Pemex station across the street."

"I know the place," I said. "Did he drive to your office?"

"Yeah," she said. "He pulled up out front by the door."

"Remember what was he driving?"

"A white SUV," she said. "I'm not good with cars. I don't know what kind it was."

If I wasn't so damn cool, I would have said, "Aha!" The trio I followed the other night drove a white SUV.

"Was he interested in property in any particular area?"

"He didn't say, but I got the impression that San Lucas was more his style. The only thing he was specific about was having a view and being close to the beach. Of course, practically everywhere here is close to the beach."

"What was he wearing?"

She took another drink, leaned forward with her elbows on the bar, lowered her head into her hands and closed her eyes, trying to reconstruct the scene in her mind.

Without opening her eyes, she said, "Tan shorts, flip-flops and a white T-shirt."

"You're pretty good," I said. "Do you know if he bought from somebody else, or talked to anybody else?"

"I have no idea. I never even got his name."

"Can you think of anything else, anything at all?"

She thought about it and shook her head.

I wrote my cell phone number on the flyer, along with the hotel number.

"If he contacts you again, or if you think of something else you've forgotten, please call me," I said. "If I'm not in, leave a message where you can be reached and I'll get back to you as soon as I can."

"You don't have a card?" she asked. "What kind of private detective doesn't have a card?"

"Hey, did the Shadow hand out business cards?" I said.

"How did that *ever* escape my mind?" she said, smacking her forehead.

She gave me one of her cards. It said that her name was Dottie Winthrop and she promised the most professional service in Los Cabos.

"I hope you mean professional *real estate* service," I said.

She laughed like she really meant it. The barrier between us was gone now that she knew I wasn't trying to pick her up and we'd become co-conspirators.

"I guess you'll never know," she said. "Now can you tell me why you're looking for him?"

I did.

"What a scumbag!" she snarled. "I bet he can't even get it up unless the woman's unconscious."

"I wouldn't know about that, but he is not a nice man, that's for sure," I agreed.

It was time to go. I slid off the bar stool.

"It was nice talking to you, Dottie Winthrop," I said. "Enjoy your dinner."

She gave me her hand.

"I like you, too," she said, holding my hand longer than necessary. "And you know, that line, as bad as it was, just might have worked."

I grinned at her. "I'm flattered."

"You should be," she said.

CHAPTER 20

THE NEXT MORNING I decided to go for a jog while I waited for Tony Suarez to show up. Dressed in Nike running shoes, red tennis shorts and no shirt, I walked down the steps, around my building and past the pool on the way down to the beach.

There were no clouds and a light breeze wafted in off the ocean. It was low tide, except for a few seabirds I was alone, and there was plenty of beach to run on.

It went well enough at first. It always does. But after about a half mile I remembered why I hated to jog. It was boring as hell and damned hard work, especially on the beach. The more I ran the deeper into the sand my feet seemed to sink.

One of my favorite movie lines comes from "The Untouchables." Sean Connery plays a veteran Chicago cop who goes on temporary assignment with Eliot Ness' squad that's trying to bring down Al Capone. When they find out that a load of illegal liquor is scheduled to cross the Canadian border, Ness and his men intercept it. Connery is chasing one of the smugglers on foot when he gets tired of the chase, fires his gun and growls, "That's enough of this running shit."

That pretty much captures how I feel about jogging. The problem is that I must be too dumb to remember because every so often I have to be reminded how much I hate it.

After another half mile I turned around. By now I was laboring badly and practically blinded by my own sweat. Despite gasping and wheezing like a heart attack was imminent, I was determined not to stop until I got back to the pool. At the same time I cursed myself for being so stubborn. As I drew closer to the hotel complex, I decided that the steps leading to the pool was close enough. After a few more strides I decided that a little way from the steps leading to the pool would do. Then I decided that right where I was would be just fine. Gasping for air, I stopped, bent over and put my hands on my knees. Feeling weak in the legs, after a couple of minutes I wobbled slowly up the steps. I considered falling into the pool but I was afraid that I didn't have enough strength to keep myself from drowning.

The pool attendant was fishing junk out of the water with a skimmer. He heard me before he saw me. He turned around, took one look and said, "Mister, are you all right?"

"Hell, no, I'm not all right." I struggled to speak between gulps of air. "Do I look like a man who's all right?"

"Want for me me to call for the doctor?"

"No, I asked for it," I said, waving him aside.

I stumbled up to my room, stripped off my soaked clothes and took a shower. I promised myself that I'd never jog again, but I knew that sooner or later I'd break that promise. It's one thing to be an idiot, but it's a terrible feeling to *know* you're an idiot.

Feeling refreshed but oh so foolish, I drove into town,

found a little restaurant, ate a lot of things that were bad for me and drove back to the hotel.

I'd just closed the door to my room when the telephone rang.

"Hello."

"Mister Cruickshank?"

"Yes."

"It's Tony Suarez. I just checked in. I'm in my room now."

"Did everything go all right?"

"Slick as can be."

"What room are you in?" I asked.

"Three twenty four," he said.

"I'll be there in a minute."

I got there at the same time one of the hotel staff was wheeling a room service cart through the door.

"I hope you don't mind," Suarez asked. "I didn't eat this morning and I'm kind of hungry."

"Not at all," I said. "While you're here just charge whatever you need to the room."

I took a look at my new partner while he signed the tab and the room service waiter fussed around. He had a lot of his father in him, but it was in a much younger and fitter package. He was one of those people you can tell is in spectacular shape just by the way they move. He looked very alert and moved lightly on his feet as if he were a baseball shortstop ready to break in any direction. His black hair had grown out from his police cut. His dark blue pullover shirt was tucked into khaki trousers with a black weave belt. The shirt was the kind that gathered at the biceps. He wore a gold Seiko watch on his left wrist, which meant that he probably was right-handed. He gave the impression of precision so exact that there was no wasted motion. It was as if every movement was planned to do exactly what it did in the most economical way possible.

"Do you mind if we go out on the balcony?" he asked.

"Sure," I said, following him outside through the sliding glass door.

He'd ordered a steak sandwich, fries and iced tea. He spread it out on a small bistro table while I took a chair to the right.

"Did your elephant gun get through okay," I asked.

Suarez grinned. "A man named Espada met me at the airport and took care of everything."

"Good," I said.

"Are there any changes in the situation since we talked?" he asked.

I told him about my unexpectedly successful conversation last night with Dottie Winthrop.

I decided to test him a little.

"What do you think?" I asked.

He took a bite of his sandwich and thought it over.

"I'd say that once Rosa talked to her he realized that he'd have to give out more information than he wanted to in order to buy a place personally," he said. "He probably thought it'd be easier in Mexico, especially for somebody paying cash. Whatever the reason, he wound up buying through a corporation that he either already had, or created soon after. Probably already had."

"Yeah, that's what I think, too," I said.

"But why buy at all?" he said. "I'm no expert, but there must be a million places to rent down here. Why leave a trail?"

That had occurred to me, too.

"Maybe he thinks he's so brilliant that nobody would figure out that he's here," I suggested. "From what I know of Rosa, he's arrogant enough to think that he's really that smart. Or, for all I know, maybe he wants to make money in real estate, not that he needs anymore money. A lot of people get into real estate down here. It's hard to go wrong. Hell, maybe it's both."

As he ate, Suarez's eyes moved from me to the ocean to a couple of young ladies who'd come down to the pool and were setting up just below his balcony. Once they arranged the lounge chairs exactly the way they wanted, they slathered themselves with sun block in the most lascivious possible way. Just watching them do it was an erotic experience. They also renewed my faith in the thong as appropriate pool attire on certain bodies.

It was safe to assume that the girls didn't give a damn what I thought. The little show was for Suarez. They knew he was watching, he knew they knew he was watching, they knew he knew that they knew it, and so it goes in the dance that never ends. At the same time, the steak sandwich was disappearing fast.

"What are our assets?" he asked.

"Good question," I said. "There's me and now there's you, and they don't know about you. They don't know that we know what they look like and where they live. There's a local cop named Valencia who's cooperative and likes us more than he doesn't like us, though it's a close call, and there's a mysterious general named Urrea who's on our side and seems to have a lot of clout."

Suarez polished off the sandwich, drained the last of his iced tea and wiped his hands on a napkin.

"What do you want me to do?" he asked.

"The surfer dude knows what I look like, so I want you to follow him," I said. "I'll take the others. When they split up I'll pick one and follow them."

"Mister Cruickshank, there's one other thing you should know before we get started," he said.

"What's that?"

"I'm gay," he said. "I just thought you should know. If

you have a problem with it, tell me now so we don't waste a lot of time."

"I probably wouldn't admit it if I did, but I don't," I said. "And didn't I just see you staring at those oily young things down there? They put on quite a show and it sure as hell wasn't for me."

He shrugged. "Sure I looked. So did you. They're good looking people."

"Yes they are, but I guess they're not on your, ah, team," I said.

"You saw that 'Seinfeld' episode, too," he said.

"I think everybody has, or at least they've heard about it and think they saw it," I said. "Anyway, it's no problem."

"Pop said you'd say that. He said you'd mean it, too. But I wanted to be upfront about it."

"Was it a problem for Chango?" I asked. "Feel free to tell me it's none of my business."

Suarez looked out over the pool toward the ocean.

"For a long time, yeah, it was a problem," he said. "Latin machismo and all that. It's okay now, though. We worked through it."

"I bet it was a lot of work," I said. "I've known your father for a long time. What about the cops? How tough was it?"

"In San Francisco?" he laughed. "Are you kidding?"

"I withdraw the question," I said. "Like Woody Allen said, at least it doubles your chances of getting a date on Saturday night."

"I'm gay, not bisexual."

"My mistake," I said. "And will you please stop calling me Mr. Cruickshank."

"Okay … Ethan," he said.

CHAPTER 21

WE SPENT the next few days watching like hell. Wherever they went, we went. As time passed, we honed watching into an art form. As watchers go, we were the A team. Nobody did it better. But for all we accomplished we might as well have been bird watchers seeking the Swizzle Nosed Peregrine.

Patience, Cruickshank, patience, I told myself. This could go on for weeks. As usual, I didn't listen to good advice. I was bored and lonesome. I'd come to like Tony Suarez a lot, but he was not Dina. I missed my girl. I missed my dog, too. I missed everything. The fact that my home was just up the road only made it worse. I was frustrated, cranky and needed to make something happen.

I was watching the resort where the girl and the two guys were staying. The guys, who turned out to be surly looking red-haired twins, left about mid-morning. Judging by their equipment, they were going scuba diving. I decided not to follow because if they split up I could only tail one. Anyway it seemed unlikely that they were planning to meet Rosa somewhere underwater. I decided to stick with the girl. So far, she hadn't done anything remotely interesting, but neither had anyone else.

Not long after the twins left, she walked out of the condo with a beach bag hanging off one shoulder. She was wearing light blue shorts, a white blouse, sandals, and extra large sunglasses with blue frames. As I followed at a safe distance, she strolled past two of the resort's smaller swimming pools to the main pool, which was larger than Lake Tahoe and shaped like a giant kidney with a waterfall at one end. She assessed the empty chairs and found one she liked that faced the beach beneath the shade of a palm tree. She took off her shorts and top to reveal a one-piece bathing suit that matched her sunglasses. After slathering herself with sun block, she took a reclining position in the chair, made three telephone calls during which her body language indicated that she was giving orders, put the phone away, and began to read some paper work she pulled out of her beach bag.

A young man dressed like all the rest of the resort staff with a white pullover shirt and black shorts asked if I needed a pool towel. I waved him off and went back to the condo. What I was about to do was crazy, but why should that stop me? I was going to break into her condo to see what I could find. It was either that or hang around and watch her get a tan.

The right way to do it was to position Suarez somewhere outside so he could warn me in case the twins or the girl came back while I was inside. But I wanted to do it now and nothing was going to stop me. It was unbelievably reckless, not to mention remarkably stupid. And I didn't give a damn.

After looking around to make sure that no one was

watching, I picked the lock of the condo door in less than thirty seconds and walked in, shutting the door behind me. I could tell that the place was empty the minute I opened the door. There's a peculiar stillness to an empty place that doesn't feel like anything else. I felt a tingling in my groin, the same feeling I had as a kid playing hide and seek, and caught myself holding my breath. Some things don't change. In the silence, the faint hum of the refrigerator sounded like a roar. As pumped up as I was, it was as if I could feel the passing of nano seconds. I locked the door and went to work.

It was a one-bedroom condo with a spectacular view of beach and ocean. The door leading to the twins' place next door was to my left, just beyond the small kitchen. The door was locked from this side, so I was safe from interruption there. The rest of the condo consisted of a combination living room-dining room separated from the kitchen by a tile counter, and a bedroom and bathroom to the right. Both the living room and bedroom had floor-to-ceiling sliding glass doors leading to a large balcony.

Usually the only part of the kitchen that reveals anything other than eating habits is the trash, which was located in the usual place under the sink. It was absolutely empty. There wasn't much food in the refrigerator; half a cantaloupe, a few eggs, orange juice, a bottle of sparkling water, a few vegetables, a half-empty bottle of white wine and a bag of lettuce. There was a bottle of cognac on the counter next to two bottles of red wine, and some just-add-water oat meal. A skillet, one plate, a knife, a fork and a coffee cup were in the sink, probably her breakfast dishes. Whoever she was, she was no gourmet.

The living-dining room didn't seem to have anything personal in it, just the furniture and nick-knacks that came with the place. The television was connected to a VCR and a DVD player, but there were no tapes or DVDs that I could see. The ashtrays had no traces of ash in them. There was nothing to read; not a book, a magazine, or a newspaper.

I continued my search in the bedroom. The bed was king-size. There was a dresser and mirror against the opposite wall. The wall facing the beach was taken up by the sliding door. The bathroom was on the opposite side of the room from the slider, with a closet, a double sink and make-up area, plus separate rooms for the toilet and the shower. Judging by the tangled pile of green floss in the bathroom wastebasket, she was scrupulous about dental hygiene. Dina was a dedicated flosser, too. I should floss, but never did. It was too much trouble. Someday all my teeth would fall out and I'd have only myself to blame.

I opened the closet by sliding the lacquered brown wood door to the left. There were ten pairs of shoes on the top shelf, all perfectly aligned and grouped from informal on the left to dressy on the right. The blouses, skirts, and slacks were arranged with geometric precision. Everything was hung perfectly in their proper groupings. A gourmet she wasn't, but she certainly was organized. Her dirty clothes were in a wicker basket on the closet floor; blouse, shorts, panties and bra. The safe was in the closet, too. I decided to hold that until later. It probably wouldn't take long to crack, but I didn't want to spend the time right now.

In the bathroom, the toothpaste tube was neatly rolled up from the bottom. The electric toothbrush was next to the toothpaste and the water pic was next to the electric toothbrush, which was next to the hair dryer. The medicine cabinet held deodorant, a box of tampons, band-aids, mouthwash, floss, aspirin, and various ointments and unguents. The cabinet drawers had brushes, combs and makeup, lots and lots of makeup.

I returned to the bedroom and began going through the dresser drawers. The top drawer was the underwear drawer. She had a large collection of thongs and bikini panties on one side and bras on the other, with a divider in the middle. The bras were either black or a neutral color. She appeared to be a thirty six D. How nice for her. The thongs and panties were bold colors. She could go for at least a month and not wear the same panties. At the bottom of the panties I found two plastic bags containing marijuana and cocaine, along with the accouterments used in free basing.

The nightstands on either side of the bed were identical, with a single drawer at the top and an open space underneath the drawer. I went over to the nightstand closest to the sliding glass door because that's the side of the bed where I'd sleep if I lived here, which meant that if I kept anything in one of the drawers it probably would be that one.

I opened the drawer and hit the Mother Lode, starting with a Beretta Tomcat, a thirty two caliber automatic. I thought she was carrying a gun in her purse the first time I saw her that night in the plaza and now I was sure of it. I moved the Beretta aside and found four passports and an appointment book with a faux leather cover. Four passports? Your typical marijuana-smoking, cocaine using, panties-abundant fair maid doesn't need four passports. I flipped through the passports, one by one. They were all issued within the last year; one Mexican, one American, one Colombian, and one Italian, each with a different name. The Mexican passport gave her name as Estrella Hernandez, the American passport gave her name as Mary Stratton, the Colombian passport gave her name as Maria Rosaria, and the Italian passport gave her name as Isabella Sabatini.

I copied the names and pertinent information and carefully put the passports back where I found them. It was sloppy of her to keep her passport collection anywhere but in the safe, not to mention her marijuana and cocaine stash. Over-confidence will get you every time.

I went through the leather appointment book page by page. It was small, the kind you can keep in a pocket or a purse. There weren't any names, just times, initials, Spanish words I couldn't read, mostly because her handwriting was terrible, and occasionally a longish series of numbers that might be telephone numbers, although it was impossible to tell, especially if they were South American or European numbers. In short, it was the kind of daily flotsam and jetsam you find in appointment books everywhere. If the content of her appointment book was an accurate reflection, her life lately was not action packed. From what I'd seen the last few days I believed it, too, although nobody writes down everything they do.

One entry two days from now said, "A – 2:30." Interesting. For all I knew, "A" stood for aardvark, or perhaps Achilles. Anchovy was a possibility, too. Maybe she was planning to order a pizza? But it was also possible that "A" stood for Andy or Andrew. In the silence of the empty rooms, keyed up by the fact that I'd committed a crime by being here, I could feel the adrenalin pumping through my body. What I had in my hand was an honest to God clue that might lead me to the man I was looking for. After a couple of deep breaths to settle down, I put the appointment book back where I found it underneath the passports and the Beretta.

Just as I closed the nightstand drawer, I heard a key

working in the front door. Fortunately, the sliding glass door was unlocked. I eased through it, quietly shut the door behind me and was standing with my back against the space between the slider in the bedroom and the slider in the living room before whoever it was opened the door and walked in.

CHAPTER 22

WHOEVER IT WAS WALKED into the bedroom. I could hear sandals make a slapping sound on the tile floor, which told me it probably was the girl because she wore sandals to the pool.

If she walked out on the balcony I'd have to knock her down then dash through the condo and out the door and hope she didn't get a good look at me. As plans go, it was worse than putrid. Even if it worked, it would alarm the merry little group Suarez and I were tailing. But while putting her down and running like hell wasn't a great choice, there might not be another one available to me.

When she didn't come out to the balcony, I risked a quick peek into the bedroom. She had taken off her bathing suit and was standing naked in front of the bathroom mirror, putting her hair up, her bathing suit pooled at her feet. If my situation hadn't been so precarious I would have appreciated the view more than I did. Mostly I was hoping she'd take a shower so I could sneak through the condo and out the front door before she knew I was here.

I pulled my head back, waited a moment, and risked another peek. She was at the dresser. She'd already put on a bra. She pulled out a pair of red panties and stepped into them with her back to me, pulling them tight across her nicely shaped butt.

It was a great show but I couldn't wait much longer. I had to find a way out. Jumping from this balcony to the next one was out of the question because the building was slightly curved and I couldn't see the balconies on either side. I couldn't go up either. It was too far. I couldn't reach it even if I stood on the railing.

My only choice was down. Unfortunately, I have a problem with heights. I've had it all my life. Dina and I were in Barcelona once. There's a tall monument at the waterfront with a statue of Christopher Columbus on the top. He's supposed to be pointing to the New World, but he's actually pointing toward Africa. He didn't know where he was going in 1492, and he doesn't know where he's pointing today. We took the elevator up to the observation area at the top of the monument. I should have known better. As soon as we got off the elevator I was in trouble. It was only a few feet from the inner wall to the outer glass wall but there was a slight down slope and I immediately had the sensation of falling. I turned and clung to the inner wall like Spiderman, keeping my face pressed against the wall and my back to the terrifying view. Inch by inch, I eased along the wall, making for the down elevator on the other side of the observation deck, brushing aside other tourists as I passed. I never let go of that wall, convinced that it was the only thing saving me from certain death. There was a line waiting to get on the elevator but this was no time for social pleasantries. I bulled my way through the line, jumped through the elevator doors as soon as they opened and was transported to safety on the ground below. The people I shoved aside on the way to the elevator probably still talk about that rude American in Barcelona.

But that was nothing compared to what I faced now. This time I really could fall. Barcelona was the illusion of danger. This was the real thing. Concentrating on not looking down from my fifth floor perch, but all too aware of how high I was, I swung one leg and then the other over the aluminum railing. The balcony's concrete floor was about a foot thick. I crouched facing the sliding doors with my feet supported by the four inches of concrete that extended beyond the railing. I slid my hands down the railing supports until they were just above my feet, with my fanny hanging out over the edge. I carefully moved one foot off the balcony, then the other. The second my foot left the edge my hands slid to the bottom of the railing and the sudden jolt of my two hundred and ten pounds as I dangled in the air nearly jerked my arms from my shoulders. It was all I could do to hang on to the railing as the edge of the cement floor gouged into my forearms.

Ignoring the pain in my shoulders and arms, I swung my legs back and forth as my stomach cramped with fear, trying to get enough momentum to put me on the balcony below once I released my hold. I had to let go soon because my hands and arms couldn't take the strain much longer and it felt like the rough concrete edge was grinding the inside of my forearms to hamburger.

When I finally let go I overcompensated. As I fell I could tell that my feet were too far in front. They hit a chair and the chair skittered across the balcony from the force of the blow. I hit the floor flat on my back and felt the back of my head whiplash against the concrete with a brutal thud.

The next thing I knew I was curled in a fetal position. It took a few seconds before I remembered where I was. Lying still, I took inventory of my body parts. Nothing seemed broken. I gently touched the back of my head and my fingers came away bloody. After several deep breaths, I forced myself to get up. If there was someone in this condo I was still in trouble. They'd probably already called the police.

Swaying on my feet, I peered through the sliding glass door. It was the same set-up as the condo above. I looked through both doors and didn't see anyone.

I was safe for the moment, but only that. My situation was only a little better than what I faced above. I was trapped on a fourth floor balcony with no place to go. I didn't want to repeat what I'd just gone though. Even if I was able to do it again and get down to the third floor I couldn't count on the people below not being home, not to mention the people below them and the people below them. My luck would run out sooner or later.

I tried the sliding doors. They were locked. I had to do something and do it now. If someone was staying here they could come back any time. I picked up one of the balcony chairs and threw it at the glass. It bounced off. I picked up the chair again, backed against the railing and got a running start with all my weight behind it. All I could do was hope that the slider was made of tempered glass. If it wasn't, and I succeeded in running through the door, the falling glass shards could slice me up pretty badly.

The door shattered with a boom and I stumbled into the bedroom still holding the chair in my hands. Thousands of tiny pieces of glass no bigger than a BB rained down on my head and shoulders. Let's hear it for tempered glass.

I dropped the chair on the bedroom floor. Anyone who heard the noise would have a hard time telling from which direction it came. Chances are they wouldn't recognize it either. It probably didn't sound like anything they'd heard before. I tore through the condo like a tornado, trying to be as messy and destructive as I could. I wanted it to look like an amateurish, garden-variety burglary. When the story spread around the resort as it inevitably would, when the girl heard about it she wouldn't get suspicious.

I found two hundred and fifty American dollars in one of the dresser drawers and stuffed it in my pocket. I hated to do it, but a real burglar wouldn't let the money pass. The resort would probably make it up to the occupants anyway. I didn't see anything else worth taking. I grabbed a knife from the kitchen and scratched at the closet safe as if I'd tried to get in but couldn't. I worked the knife into the crack between the safe and where it fitted into the wall, leaned against it and snapped off the blade. I let the hilt fall to the floor and left the blade stuck in the crack. I picked up the hilt, wiped it off with my shirt tail and put it back on the floor. I did the same with the chair I'd used to break the sliding door. I wanted no fingerprints. When the police saw it they'd probably assume that I'd tried to open the safe with a knife and gave up when the blade broke.

I opened the condo door and peeked out. Nobody there. I wiped the door knob with my shirt tail. Forcing myself not to run, I shut the door behind me and walked down the hall to the stair well and down two flights of stairs. I cut across an open elevated walkway and then turned right toward the main swimming pool where there were a lot of people. If anyone remembered me they'd place me here, where I was one among many.

I left the pool, walked through the resort lobby, got to my car and drove away. At least I think I did. I didn't remember any of it. The next thing I knew I was back in my room at the Hotel Sol. My back, shoulders and arms hurt and there was a great big bloody knot on the back of my head.

CHAPTER 23

I CALLED the psychiatrist about an hour later. His secretary said he was with a patient, but promised that he'd call back as soon as he could.

I waited in my room, my forearms wrapped in towels soaked in cold water. Forty five minutes later the telephone rang.

"Hello."

"Ethan?"

"Yes."

"You called?" he asked.

"Yeah." I said.

"What's going on?"

"A lot," I said. "I had an episode. Maybe two of them in a short time. I'm not sure."

"What happened?" he asked. "Tell me about it."

"Do you have time?"

"Absolutely," he said.

I told him what happened.

"I'm not sure the first one was an episode," I said. "I might have been knocked out when I hit the floor."

"That could be,' he said. "How did you feel when you came out of it?"

"Weak," I said. "Sick and weak. My head hurt. My heart was pounding."

"What about the other one?"

"I'm sure that one was an episode," I said. "I don't remember a thing."

"How do you feel now?"

"Mostly I'm ashamed of myself," I said.

"What do you mean?"

"I was so damn stupid," I explained. "Breaking into the girl's place the way I did wasn't very professional. I should have waited for back-up but I did it anyway. Maybe I've lost it? Hell, maybe I never had it to lose? Maybe I ought to do everybody a favor and give it up?"

"Ethan, I'm no expert at that kind of thing, but I'd say, yes, you should have waited," he said. "You've always been too impulsive. But that doesn't mean you've lost anything. One poor decision doesn't make you're a failure. I don't think that giving up would be good for you now."

There was a pause on the other end. I didn't say anything either.

"For what it's worth," he said. "I don't think the first time was an episode. It does sound like you were knocked out."

"And the other?"

"That almost certainly *was* an episode," he said. "I'm not surprised, given the stressful situation. This is all conjecture, of course, but what I suspect might have happened is that without being aware of it you managed to fight off the disassociation until the crisis passed. You knew that having an episode at that time would put you in even more danger than you were already in. You certainly did not want to have a dis-associative episode while dangling from the balcony. Do you remember having any symptoms?"

"No, but there was a lot going on at the time," I said. "You almost sound encouraged."

"In a way, I suppose I am," he said.

"Then why do I feel so damn lousy?" I asked.

I could tell that he was thinking as he talked, trying to put the pieces together faster than he wanted to, without the advantage of body language and nuance. He didn't want to commit himself to something that he'd have to take back later, or something that might lead me down the wrong track.

"What happened shows that you may have more control over the disassociation than we thought, at least at some times, and that's for the good," he said. "It's difficult to draw conclusions this quickly, but I'm fairly sure I'm right. You're discouraged because you feel that you behaved badly. You're facing this alone, you didn't go into it with a lot of confidence, and what happened obviously eroded it. But that doesn't mean you're a failure. Everybody makes poor decisions sometimes. There will be lows just as there will be highs. That's called life."

"Do you make poor decisions?" I asked.

"Ethan, you have no idea," he said.

We talked for more than an hour. He'd bill me, of course, but I knew that he'd only bill me for an hour. For all I knew, he had fifty people beating at his door, but he never seemed rushed. It was as if he had nothing better in the world to do than to talk to me for as long as I needed it. Therapy by telephone wasn't as good as face to face, but it was a lot better than nothing.

"Have you told Dina?" he asked.

"I haven't had a chance," I replied. "It just happened. I called you first."

"What about the other?"

"What other?"

"Stop it, Ethan," he said.

He didn't scold me often, but when he did I knew that he meant it.

"You know what I mean. A man tried to kill you and you had to kill him. You're in danger down there and apparently you've refused to talk about it to the person who means the most to you. You know that your lifelong habit of repression is one of the causes of your disassociation, going back to the death of your parents. We've been working on that for years. You've got to tell Dina. You've simply *got* to talk about it or everything we've done is wasted."

"I told you," I protested. "You and I are talking about it."

The words sounded ridiculous even as I said them. I was trying to defend the indefensible. It was weak and I knew it.

"That's not what I mean," he said. "You owe it to yourself and you owe it to her."

"What good would it to?" I asked. "It would only frighten her unnecessarily. With her father, she has enough problems right now."

"Ethan, I'd hoped that we were beyond that," he said. "Dina has earned the right to worry about you. Sharing the good and the bad is part of what being a couple is all about. You need to get it out and you need to share it with her. It will be good for you and, difficult as it might be, it will reassure Dina that you're including her in your life, although she won't like it that you've held back. The longer you wait, the harder it will be to tell her. Look at it this way, if your positions were reversed, wouldn't you want her to tell you? It won't be easy, but it must be done."

I didn't answer right away. I was too busy stewing in my own thoughts.

"All right," I admitted. "You've got me."

He could hear the reluctance in my voice and pressed harder.

"I mean it, Ethan," he said. "This could be a serious setback if you don't follow through. No one can do it for you. Saying that you're trying to protect her is just another excuse."

"I'll tell her," I said. "I promise. It's gonna be hard, though."

"There's no doubt of that," he agreed. "If you'd like, call me after you talk to Dina."

"I don't know if I'll be able to," I said. "I'm not exactly on a schedule down here."

"Then call when you can," he said. "If I'm not available, I'll get back to you as soon as possible. One way or another, we'll connect."

"Okay," I said. "Thanks, doc."

I hung up the phone.

"Bastard," I said.

CHAPTER 24

It was too late to call Dina right away. It was late at night in France. I waited until the next morning.

Part of me hoped that she wasn't there. Maybe she was out somewhere? It would be a reprieve. I could say that I tried, then go on my way.

My hope was shot to hell when Dina answered the telephone.

"Bonjour."

"Bonjour yourself, kid," I said.

"Why, hello, sweetie," she said. "What a nice surprise."

"I was hoping you'd feel that way," I said. "How are you doing?"

"Except for you not being here, not bad. Daddy's home."

She talked for a while about her father, how happy he was to be home and how he even looked pretty good, although he was weak and needed a lot of help. She didn't say that he looked pretty good for a man who was dying by inches, but we both knew that's what she meant.

"Kid, I've got something to tell you," I said. "I wasn't

entirely truthful the last time I called. I haven't told you everything that's happened here. I didn't lie exactly, but, well, you know."

"You've been talking to your doctor, haven't you?" she asked.

"Yeah," I admitted.

"And he made you call me?"

"I wouldn't say he *made* me do anything."

"Okay, he urged you to call and tell me whatever it was you didn't tell me before, is that about it?" she said.

"Yeah, I guess so," I admitted.

"So tell me now."

I told her everything I should have told her before about the guy I'd found in my room and how I had to shoot him. I told her about Tony Suarez, and about what happened yesterday, including dangling from the balcony and the dissociation on the way back to my hotel.

"Are you okay?" she asked.

"Yeah," I said. "My arms are a little messy and I've got a big knot on the back of my head, but other than that I'm fine."

"What will you do now?" she asked.

"I don't know," I said. "I feel like I've been improvising ever since I started this thing. I'm gonna see what "A" at two thirty means, though."

Dina was quiet while she absorbed it all. Her silence was worse than if she'd yelled at me.

"Ethan, do you think they'll ever come a time when you can just tell me things on your own, without someone forcing you to do it?" she asked.

"Yes, I do. It'll happen. I know it will."

"But when? How long do we go on like this?"

It tore me up. She shouldn't have to ask for anything, especially not from me. It shouldn't be a problem. But there it was. And it was my fault. Sure, there were reasons why I was the way I was, but it doesn't take much for reasons to turn into excuses. I'd taken the easy way out. I always had good intentions, at least that's what I told myself, but unless I was forced I almost always found an excuse to wiggle out.

"Dina, I'm sorry," I said. "I know I'm an idiot and you deserve better from me. I promise that I'll try. Changing how I've been my whole life is hard and I'm not doing it very well. Hang in there with me, kid. I need you."

"You can't help what happened," she said. "And I'm sorry I came on so strong. You can't help the way you are."

"But I'm learning, at least I'm trying to," I said. "I'm just not learning real fast."

"I love you," she said. "Please don't forget that."

"Oh, boy, do I love you, too," I said. "Don't you forget that."

CHAPTER 25

I DECIDED to do a two-man tail on the girl when she did whatever she was going to do about the mysterious A. It probably would be better to have Suarez tail her alone because the other side didn't know what he looked like, but if A turned out to be Andy Rosa I wanted to see him for myself.

We returned the motorcycle and got Tony a rental car, a little Toyota, and put together a plan: While I waited in the parking lot of a small strip of offices and shops across the highway from the resort entrance, Tony went into the resort to keep an eye on the condo so we'd know when she left. It could be that A was just supposed to call her at two thirty, or she was supposed to call A, but I doubted it. A telephone call isn't the kind of thing people make notes about.

One complication was that we didn't know where the meeting was going to take place, assuming there was a meeting. For all we knew it might be on adjoining inner tubes out in the Pacific. That explained why we were on the job bright and early after putting the girl to bed late the night before. Feeling stiff and grumpy from not enough sleep, after basting in my car since six that morning my cell phone rang at one forty five.

"She's on her way," Suarez said.

A few minutes later I saw the white SUV pull out of the resort entrance and turn right onto the highway, with Suarez not far behind. She was by herself. Relieved to finally be doing something, I pulled out of the parking lot and followed Suarez. It looked like she was either headed to San Jose del Cabo or to the airport. I stayed far enough back so that I could see Suarez, but not her.

After a leisurely drive up the coast it turned out to be the airport. Suarez called to say that she'd parked into the lot in front of the terminal. Pulling into the lot, which was about half full, I spotted Suarez's car two rows back and to the right of the SUV. I circled the lot and parked in the same row as Suarez but on the other side of the SUV at the end of the row near the exit.

As I got out of the Focus, I saw Suarez walk into the terminal across the street. I looked around as left the parking lot, but there didn't seem to be anybody watching for a tail on the girl.

Inside the bustling terminal I strolled up to the board that displays the times of incoming flights like I was meeting somebody when my cell phone rang again.

"It looks like she's meeting a flight from Mexico City," Suarez said. "It was due at two thirty but it's posted to arrive at two fifty now."

I found the flight on the board while I listened to Suarez on the telephone.

"Where is she?" I asked.

"She's sitting in a chair near where the passengers come out after they've picked up their luggage," he said. "White shorts and a red blouse."

In case anyone was watching, I checked my watch and shook my head as if to indicate my irritation over the fact that the flight I was waiting for was late. I sauntered over to the usual airport stall that sold everything from magazines to candy bars. I had my sunglasses on, so I didn't have to be very sneaky to spot her. She was reading a paperback. The white shorts showed off her legs. Her dark hair was pulled back and the style suited her. Her features were sharp enough for a nice clean look without being too sharp. It made her look younger, too. Her various passports all had the same birth date. Assuming it really was her birth date she was only twenty eight. She was a hell of a good looking woman.

"Got her," I said. "Where are you?"

"Directly across from her," he said.

I left the stall and walked out into the crowded terminal. Most of the tourists waiting for their flights home looked happy, tanned and slightly wasted from their vacation in Los Cabos. Having all that fun can wear you out. I saw Suarez lounging in one of the airport chairs with one ankle hiked up on the other knee. He had a Spanish language newspaper in one hand and held his cell phone to his ear with the other hand. He had my digital camera, too. If Rosa had changed his look we wanted to get a picture of it. Before we left this morning Suarez cut a hole through the newspaper for the camera lens. It was a crude setup, but I'd used it often enough to know that it worked.

"I see you," I said.

I looked around the terminal, searching for the best position.

"See the bar in the middle of the terminal?" I said.

"Yes."

"I'm going to sit there and have a beer," I said. "I'll be able to see you both and still be part of a crowd."

I didn't want a beer, but ordering one didn't mean I had to drink it. I walked to the bar, slid onto a stool and ordered a Bohemia. On the board, it said that the arrival of the flight from Mexico City had been pushed back again, this time to three fifteen. To keep up appearances, I took a sip of my beer. I changed my mind about not wanting it. After sitting for more than seven hours in a hot car, it tasted pretty good.

At three twenty, first in Spanish and then in English, the usual barely understandable airport voice announced that the flight from Mexico City was arriving at gate two. The girl dog-eared a page of her paperback, closed it, put it in her purse, got up and walked a few steps to where the passengers would enter the terminal. Judging by the number of people who were meeting the flight, it looked like it was full, or close to it. Suarez put down one section of the newspaper and picked up another one.

Ten minutes later, Andy Rosa walked into the terminal. I was glad that I had my sunglasses on because I was staring hard. After all this time, it was almost as if I didn't believe it was really him. I felt clammy and a little dizzy as my heart thumped in my chest.

He was wearing jeans, a white pullover shirt, and sandals, with a burgundy leather carry-on bag slung over one shoulder. Although I knew how tall he was from the description, he was still taller than I expected. He was broader across the shoulders, too. It probably came from the surfing. Like Dottie Winthrop said, he'd shaved his head and grown a goatee, but it didn't change his look as much as he probably hoped it would. He looked like Andy Rosa with a shaved head and a goatee. Even from where I was I could see the arrogant eyes that I'd come to dislike so much.

He saw her at the same time she saw him. They gave each other the kind of lingering wildly erotic kiss that lovers do early in a hot love affair, when you can barely control yourself. When they finally stopped and began to walk out of the terminal, Rosa shifted his bag to his right shoulder so that he could put his left arm around her shoulders while she put her right arm around his waist.

I felt a surprising pang of disappointment. She was slumming. I didn't know why, but I knew she was better than Andy Rosa. I didn't even have a name for her. There were too many to choose from. But the mystery only added to her dark allure.

I tossed some money on the bar for the beer and a tip. I'd just hopped off the stool when my phone rang.

"What would you call that thing tagging along behind Rosa?" Suarez asked. "A brontosaurus?"

I was so intent on the love birds that I hadn't noticed, although I didn't see how once I saw him. It was like seeing a Clydesdale at the Westminster Kennel Show. Although he was clearly accompanying Rosa, he was unacknowledged by either Rosa or the girl, and walked several paces behind. He had his own burgundy leather carry on, which, given his size, looked no bigger than a brief case. He wasn't really as big as a Clydesdale, but he was plenty big enough. My best guess put him at around six seven and three hundred and fifty pounds. He wore a sleeveless white T shirt, the better to display his stupendous arms while the shirt strained over his enormous chest. Sneakers and dark blue shorts that came down to just below his knees completed the outfit. His calves resembled pilings. He had thick black curly hair, eyebrows that ran in a dark bushy line above his eyes, and what looked like a permanent scowl; a giant version of Cro-Magnon man.

"So what do you think, protection or a pal?" I asked Suarez.

"The way they ignore him, he's protection," he replied. "A lot of it, too."

Leaving his newspaper on the chair, Suarez put on his

sunglasses and followed the trio through the automatic doors and across the street to the parking lot. Watching through the glass, I waited until the SUV pulled away before I went outside. After the cool of the terminal, the heat hit me like a blow to the face. I was sweating before I got to the car. I saw Suarez's Toyota leave the lot as I opened the door to the Focus.

With the air conditioner going full blast, I waited until we left San Jose del Cabo behind and were tooling along on the highway before I called Suarez. He was about a quarter of a mile away, with four cars between us. Whenever we went into a curve I lost sight of him.

"You still got 'em?" I asked.

"Of course, I've still got 'em," he said. "You think I'm an amateur?"

"It never crossed my mind," I said. "We old folks worry a lot. Anything interesting?"

"Nothing," he said. "The girl's driving, the brontosaurus has the passenger seat, and Rosa's in the back."

"That's the right setup for protection," I said. "If he was a pal he'd probably sit in back."

"Maybe he's just a big oaf and Rosa likes having him around because he's showy and makes Rosa feel important?" Suarez said.

"Or maybe Rosa took note of what happened to the guy in my room, decided to upgrade the help and hired him to thwart people like us," I said. "Hell, he could be a Rhodes Scholar on vacation in sunny Mexico. Still, we've got to assume that he knows what he's doing. Did you get a decent shot of Rosa?"

"Yeah, I think so," Suarez said. "By the way, if it comes down to it, feel free to take the brontosaurus on yourself. I am, after all, just a lowly employee."

"Lowly employees are always the first to be sacrificed," I said. "Call me if there's anything interesting."

The highway straightened out so I could see both Suarez and the SUV. I was mildly surprised when it didn't turn into the resort where the girl and her two pals stayed. Then I was really surprised when it didn't turn toward the place where the surfer dude was wont to dwell.

My telephone rang again.

"Where the hell are they going?" Suarez asked, echoing my own thoughts.

"I don't know," I said. "We'll find out soon enough. It won't be long before they run out of territory."

They drove through downtown, passed the marina and followed the main street as it turned left, then turned right and started up the hill into a ritzy area known as Pedregal.

I cursed to myself. We'd had it. There was a guard at the Pedregal gate house. Assuming Rosa had a place there, or knew someone who did, the SUV would sail through and we wouldn't.

Suarez and I stopped short of the Pedregal entrance while the SUV drove to the gate house and the uniformed guard stepped up to the door. After a brief conversation the barrier went up and the SUV passed through, headed up the winding cobblestone road. I drove past the entrance, made a U turn and came back down on the other side of the street.

To my surprise, I saw Suarez at the gate house. The guard came out to meet him. The guard stepped back, the barrier went up, and Suarez drove in.

My telephone rang.

"I'll meet you back at the hotel," he said.

CHAPTER 26

THE HOTEL SOL was only a couple of minutes away. I left the Ford in the parking lot and walked to my room.

I tore off my clothes and put on my bathing suit. I grabbed my cell phone and a towel, went back down the stairs, tossed towel and phone on a vacant lounge chair that faced the ocean and was shaded by a big green umbrella, and dove into the pool. The shock of the cool water felt hard and cleansing on my body. It was still a little early for the after-fishing crowd and the pool was empty except for four or five hardcore drinkers at the swim-up bar. I swam underwater to the other side of the pool, surfaced, took a deep breath and swam back again. As I swam, I reached as far as I could to stretch the muscles in my shoulders and back. The physical activity felt good after spending most of the day in my car.

After five more underwater laps, it occurred to me that I hadn't eaten since very early this morning. Suddenly I was ravenously hungry. It was too early for dinner, so I swam to the bar and ordered some shrimp tacos and two beers.

After five more laps, my arms and shoulders were aching pleasantly from the exercise. Ten laps in a big pool seemed like a good place to stop. It beat the hell out of jogging. I got out of the pool, toweled off, and collapsed in the lounge chair.

I was dozing when my shrimp tacos and beer arrived fifteen minutes later. I signed the check, added a tip, and devoured the food and beer in a fraction of the time it took to get it to me.

Replete with food and exercise, I went back to my room, tossed my bathing suit in the bathroom sink and took a long hot shower. I got out of the shower, dressed, and began rummaging through the hotel literature and the tourist book that was placed in every room to see if I could find out anything about Pedregal.

I already knew a little, but not much. Pedregal was the most upscale development in Los Cabos. I'd played tennis up there two or three times on two sunken hard courts that were shared by the development. Except for the winding streets, my impression of the place was so vague that it was barely an impression.

After finding nothing about Pedregal in the literature, it occurred to me that I had a source in the local real estate business. I found Dottie Winthrop's business card and gave her a call.

"So tell me," I said, "do you come here often?"

"Well, what do you know, it's the private eye," she said. "Don't tell me, you got a divorce and now you need lots and lots of comforting?"

"Sorry, but I'm afraid you won't win cash and prizes and move on to the next level," I said.

"Story of my life," she said. "So how's the hunt going?"

"Making progress," I said. "Have you got a minute? I need some real estate information."

"Sure," she said. "What do you need?"

"Tell me about Pedregal."

"You thinking of buying, or something?" she asked.

"The guy I was looking for came in today from Mexico City," I explained. "I followed him to Pedregal."

"Did you see which house," she asked. "I've sold a couple up there. I might know the property."

"I've got somebody on it," I said. "I'll call you when he gets back. In the meantime, tell me about the place in general."

"It takes some real money to get in there," she said. "Prices start at around seven hundred and fifty thousand for a smallish place and go up to eight or nine million. Most of the owners either live there seasonally or vacation there. A lot of them rent out the place when they're not there. Rents start at about four or five hundred a night."

"What else?" I asked.

"An architect named Rivera bought the land – about three hundred and fifty acres, I think – back in the mid seventies," she said. "It's the most dramatic piece of property in the area, high up overlooking all of Cabo San Lucas, with the city on one side and the ocean on the other. It's literally at land's end, far enough away from town to feel isolated but close enough to be convenient to everything. Once you're inside the gate, the homes are private, too. They're built so that nobody's looking at anybody else. A bunch of celebrities have bought in there over the years. Sylvester Stallone had a place for a while. I heard Mick Jagger did, too. He sold it, I think."

"He probably couldn't get no satisfaction," I said. "Besides the gate, is there any other security?"

"Nothing official," she said. "I'm sure that some of the people who live there have their own security. There are maintenance people and gardeners around every day. Some of the homes have staff, too, mostly cooks and housekeepers. There are exceptions, I suppose, but most of the help doesn't live on site."

"So they go in and out everyday?"

"Yeah."

"What about access?" I asked. "Is the main gate the only way to drive in?"

"Yep."

"Any walking access?"

"You *can* get there from the beach," she said. "In fact, it's not too far from where you're staying. There's a path so that the owners and renters can walk down to the beach. Most of the homes have fences, gates and locks. If you wanted to live private, but with easy access to everything, Pedregal's the place if you have the money."

"Can I get a map?" I asked. "The more detailed the better."

"Oh, sure," she said. "I might even have one around here somewhere. I can make a copy for you. If I don't have it, I can get it."

"You know, you're pretty good," I said.

"You bet your ass, I'm good," she said. "If you get an address let me know. If I don't know the layout I'll know where to find it."

"You'll be hearing from me," I said. "I'd appreciate it if you wouldn't tell anyone about this conversation."

"Did we have a conversation?"

"Thanks, Dottie," I said.

CHAPTER 27

I'D JUST FINISHED my talk with Dottie Winthrop when someone knocked on the door. I grabbed my gun, stepped to the door, peered through the peephole and saw Tony Suarez on the other side.

I opened the door and he walked in.

"You wouldn't happen to have a beer, would you?" he asked.

"I think I might be able to find one somewhere," I said.

I took a Pacifico out of the refrigerator and handed it to him.

"Want to go out on the balcony while we talk?" I asked.

"Sure," he said. "As long as there's shade."

We opened the sliding glass door and walked out on the balcony. The pool was more crowded than when I left it. The fishermen were back. Most of them were hanging around the swim-up bar, either sitting on the underwater bar stools or standing waist deep in water. Other tourists were standing in the pool with drinks in their hands or lounging in the chairs at poolside, cooling off from whatever they'd done during the day.

It looked like Suarez needed to cool off himself. There were dark rings of perspiration under each arm. When we walked out to the balcony, I saw a line of perspiration along his spine, too.

"Hot work?" I asked, watching him drain half his beer in one long gulp.

"There's nothing like baking in a car for most of a day to make me glad I'm going to law school," he said.

"How'd you get through the guard at the gate?" I asked.

"It helps to speak the language," he said. "But it probably had more to do with the hundred dollars I gave him."

I laughed. "Ah, yes, the universal language. What happened then?"

"I followed the SUV along a winding road, most of it up," he said. "At the top they pulled through an electric gate into a driveway. There's a ten-foot wall along the front, so I couldn't see anything. I didn't want to risk being spotted, so I didn't try to take a closer look. I got the feeling that it's a pretty big place. Unless I was screwed up from all the curves, judging by the location I think it overlooks the beach not too far from here. The view must be incredible."

"Did you get the address?" I asked.

Suarez polished off the other half of his beer and glared at me over the bottle.

"Okay," I said, raising my hand in apology, "never mind."

I asked if he wanted another beer, but he shook his head.

"I waited down the street for a while, but nobody came in or went out," he said. "I finally decided that it'd be best to come back. I had a conversation with the guard on the way out. Apparently Rosa lives there. It sounds like he left just before you got here and moved in not too long before that. The guard doesn't know if he owns the place or rents it. Although he has people in and they often spend the night as far as he knows Rosa's the only one who actually lives there. By the way, the brontosaurus is new. The guards haven't seen him before."

"That's nice work, Tony," I said. "All this time we've been looking for a guy who wasn't here."

"That means it was the rest of them who reacted to what you were doing, the flyers and everything," Suarez added.

"Could be," I agreed. "Or maybe they contacted Rosa and he issued the orders?"

"Anyway, the guard's gonna keep an eye on him for us," Suarez continued. "Nothing obvious, but if Rosa goes somewhere overnight or longer the guard'll know because security keeps tabs on the empty houses. They'll know where he's going and how long he'll be gone. The guard promised to call us."

"I assume he's not doing it for love," I said.

"The hundred a day I promised probably has something to do with it," Suarez explained. "There are three shifts of guards and they'll split it three ways. I was prepared to go higher because it's not that much money, but he sure was happy. I hope that's OK."

"For them it's a lot," I explained. "They don't make much down here. Over a week's time it's a pretty nice bonus. Probably almost equals their pay. And the money's no problem. Don't worry about it."

"By the way, they don't like Rosa," Suarez added. "They say he's an arrogant bastard who treats the help like dirt."

"That's our boy," I said. "At least he's consistent. Why

don't you go take a swim or get a shower or something while I make a call."

"I don't need much convincing for that," he said, rising from the chair. "I'll see you later."

Once he was out the door I called Dottie Winthrop again.

"How would you like to go to dinner with two handsome, suave and debonair men?" I asked.

"Sure," she said. "Know any?"

"Cute," I said. "Did you find the Pedregal map?"

"It turned out that I don't have one here, but I can get it first thing in the morning," she said.

I gave her the address that Suarez gave me.

"Think you can get the layout of the house?" I asked.

"Oh, hell yes," she said. "Let's get together tomorrow night."

"You tell me where," I said. "Expense is no object."

She named the restaurant. I knew it. She took me seriously when I said expense was no object. We settled on seven thirty. She said she'd meet us there.

"It'll save you driving all the way up to San Jose to pick me up, then taking me back after dinner," she said.

"You sure?" I asked. "We'll be more than happy to do it."

"That's okay. I'll see you tomorrow night at seven thirty."

I hadn't talked to Eddie Heenan in a while. I decided to call and tell him that we'd finally found Rosa. First, I tried the bar he owned. No luck. I struck out on his cell phone, too. I couldn't even get through to leave a message. Modern technology had foiled me again. I finally found him at his house and brought him up to date.

"Hot damn," he said. "So what's the tally? How many people does Rosa have around him?"

"There's the girl, the twins, the surfer dude, the brontosaurus, and Rosa himself," I said. "At least that's what we know about. If there's more, we haven't seen them."

"You got a plan?" he asked.

"Not yet," I said. "We only found him this afternoon. I'm going to get the layout of the house tomorrow. I'm inclined to try to grab him on the street or in the house. There are complications to both. I'll know better after tomorrow."

There was a long silence on the other end.

"Eddie?" I asked. "You still there?"

"Goddamit!" he said. "I'm coming down."

"You're what?"

"I can't stand it," he said. "I'm coming down. Sitting here with my thumb up my butt while you do all the heavy lifting is driving me crazy."

"What about your, ah, problem with the Mexican authorities?" I asked.

"To hell with 'em," he said. "I'll deal with that when I have to. If I use a phony passport and everything goes smooth they won't even know I was there. I've got a couple of things to clear up, so I can't say for sure when I'll get there. You still at the Hotel Sol?"

"Yes," I said. "But I don't know about the ID business, Eddie. If something went wrong and they grabbed you, that'd just make it worse for everybody."

"Maybe you're right," he admitted. "I'll think about it. But I'm still coming. Don't wait around for me. Do whatever you need to do and I'll find you when I get in, okay?"

"That's fine with me."

"My coming down doesn't change our deal," he said. "I've just gotta get there myself. As spectator sports go, this sucks."

"Like I said, it's fine with me. If I'm not around when

you get in, leave a message and I'll call you as soon as can."

I put the phone back in its cradle and let out a long breath. There's a lot to be said for reinforcements.

CHAPTER 28

FLAMINGO, the restaurant where we were meeting Dottie, was typical of a lot of Cabo San Lucas in that it was down a dark unpaved road that looked like it didn't led anywhere you could possibly want to go if you valued your life but it was worth it once you got there.

It was one of Los Cabos' better occasion restaurants. There was a mission-style wall around the restaurant and customers entered through an arched doorway on the street. Mexican tin lanterns hung from the palm trees in a big courtyard that featured outdoor dining and soft jazz playing in the background. A palapa covered the center of the courtyard. You could eat indoors, too, but Dina and I never did. I didn't even know what it looked like indoors. Between the lanterns and lights in the trees and the candles on the tables there was enough light to read the menus but still keep it elegantly romantic, atmosphere that would be wasted on a party consisting of one happily married man, one gay man, and one single woman. Nothing is perfect.

Dottie showed up about five minutes after we did, wearing red sandals and a white linen skirt and blouse. She walked in like she knew she was the best-looking woman there, which she was, but somehow she kept it from being offensive or overbearing, the way it would have been in most other women.

Like a lot of restaurants in Cabo, the menu was priced in dollars and pesos. I decided to celebrate and ordered a bottle of seventy five dollar champagne for the three of us. Dottie raised her glass for a toast.

"Here's to the dynamic duo and whatever in the hell you're going to do now," she said.

Suarez and I laughed. "Considering that we still don't know that's an appropriate toast," I said. "Did you get what we needed?"

"Of course," she said. "A little more, too."

"Why don't we order and then we'll go over it before dinner comes?" I suggested.

They were agreeable. I ordered a mixed green salad with vinaigrette dressing and a roasted Cornish Game Hen on a bed of sautéed mushrooms. Suarez ordered an appetizer of cheese ravioli with sun dried tomatoes and cilantro, followed by a roasted duck with a mango glaze. Dottie had baked brie in a pecan crust for an appetizer. Her entrée was blacked rock shrimp in a mango papaya sauce.

When the waiter left, Dottie reached into the vast recesses of her purse and pulled out a Pedregal map and the house layout, along with several photographs that she distributed as she talked.

"I got the photos off the internet," she said. "A previous owner used to rent out the place and pictures were still there when I went to the agency website. It's one of the best properties in Cabo, a three-level villa that's on the border between the beach and cliff side."

"The main entrance has a fountain in an enclosed courtyard. On the first level there's a fully modern kitchen with a microwave, dishwasher and breakfast bar.

The formal dining area seats six and there's seating for four on the terrace. The sunken living area opens onto the terrace with a fantastic view of the beach and the Sea of Cortez. There's also a half bathroom on that level. The second level has three master suites with very large private bathrooms. Two of the suites open onto the pool deck. As you can see, there's a cantilevered pool that overlooks the beach, complete with a swim up bar, a Jacuzzi and a private bath. There's another bar and a built-in barbecue on the terrace. The third level has the master suite. The suite opens onto a private terrace with a fountain that over looks the pool."

Dottie drained her champagne glass and held it out for a refill. Suarez reached into the ice bucket, grabbed the bottle by the neck and poured.

"That's it, guys," she said. "If I sounded too much like a real estate shill, sorry, but that's what I am. This is a hell of a nice place."

We had several questions and she answered them all. When we finished, I reached across the table, took her hand, raised it to my lips and kissed it.

"You're great," I said. "All this talent and beauty, too."

At that moment, if Dottie Winthrop had been capable of blushing she probably would have. She was a lot softer than she pretended to be. Most people are.

Our food arrived. When the waiter finally stopped fussing over us, Dottie turned her attention to Suarez.

"So what's your story, handsome," she asked. "I know about your partner here. Don't tell me that you're married with bonds of iron, too."

Now it was Suarez's turn to be self-conscious. It was the first time I'd seen him off balance. His face was frozen into an awkward half smile.

"Not exactly," he said. "I guess from your point of

view it's even worse than that. You see, the thing is … I'm gay."

Dottie's blinked, then eased back in her chair and laughed. It was a big gusty laugh from a person who knew that the joke was on her and didn't mind.

"Well I'll be damned," she said. "I'm not exactly on a hot streak, am I? The two best men I've met in a year and one way or another they couldn't be any more taken."

"Ah, but if we weren't," I said.

"Yeah, if … ," she laughed.

Our business finished, we spent the rest of dinner talking about nothing and everything. Their sexual preferences aside, Dottie and Suarez showed signs of becoming lifelong pals. By the end of the evening they were completing each others' sentences. I felt like a proud father.

It was after ten by the time we left Flamingo. Dottie gave both of us a kiss on the cheek while we said our goodbyes on the street just outside the entrance.

"You be careful on the drive back," I said. "That highway's pretty dark."

"Don't worry," she said. "I've done it a million times. I could do it in my sleep."

"That's what I'm afraid of," I said.

With a wave of her hand, Dottie walked over to her humongous, gas-guzzling Cadillac Escalade. She climbed in, made a three-point turn on the dirt road in front of the restaurant, honked goodbye and drove away.

"That's one neat lady," said Suarez.

"She sure is," I agreed.

CHAPTER 29

THE TELEPHONE JANGLED ME AWAKE. I looked at the clock on my bedside table before I answered the phone. It was just after two. I was tempted not to answer. I'd learned a long time ago that nobody calls late at night with good news. But ignoring it wouldn't make it go away. I've tried it often enough to be sure.

"Hello."

"Mister Cookshrink, please."

The voice was Mexican and heavily accented but understandable.

"This is he," I said.

"I am Doctor Oswaldo Padilla," he said. "I am calling from St. Luke's Hospital in Cabo San Lucas."

"Yes," I said.

"There is a woman here, an American. She is …" I heard the shuffling of papers, as if he had to look it up. "… Dorothy Winthrop who resides in San Jose del Cabo."

When he said Dottie's name there was a sudden tightness in my throat.

"Yes," I said again. It was all I could get out.

"She has asked for you many times," he said. "She would like you to come to the hospital."

"What happened?" I asked.

"She was brought in," he said. "She was very badly used, I'm afraid. She has been treated but refuses to be sedated until she talks to you. We can do that without her consent, of course, but I don't want to upset her more than she already is. I agreed to call you. If you were there, fine. If not, I would sedate her without her consent. Will you come?"

"I'm on my way."

"Do you know the location of the hospital?"

"Yes."

I was on the road in five minutes. St. Luke's was north of town on the road leading up the coast to Todo Santos. The streets were empty. Even Cabo San Lucas has to sleep sometime. Driving fast in a small town and ignoring the speed bumps, it only took about ten minutes to get there.

I parked in a dirt lot next to the hospital and ran inside. There was a counter along the far wall of the small lobby. I walked up to it and was met by a young lady with short dark hair, glasses with black rims, and a brisk, no nonsense attitude.

"My name is Ethan Cruickshank," I said. "Doctor Padilla called me about a friend who was brought here. Her name is Dorothy Winthrop. He asked me to come."

She frowned in that supercilious way that too many low-level administrative types seem to have perfected.

"Your name?" she asked.

"I just told you," I said. "It's Cruickshank, Ethan Cruickshank."

I spelled it while she wrote it down on a small lined yellow pad on her desk. If she'd written any more slowly she could have carved it in marble.

"And the patient's name is?" she asked.

"Dorothy Winthrop."

She started the same routine as before but I wasn't going through it again.

I reached across the counter and took away her notepad. Her jaw dropped and her mouth gaped open. She was shocked at my violation of her space. Who the hell did I think I was? Didn't I realize that she was an important person?

I hardened my eyes. "You will stop jerking around and call Doctor Padilla right now." I kept my voice to a whisper. Sometimes quiet is scarier than noisy.

She was rattled but didn't want to show it. That way, later on she could pretend that she wasn't. She picked up the telephone and punched three numbers with the eraser end of her pencil. She spoke in Spanish. The only words I recognized were "Padilla" and my name.

She listened, nodded and put the telephone back in its cradle.

Pointing with her chin toward two swinging doors to the right of the counter, she said, "Go through those doors to the end of the hall, then turn right."

"Thank you," I said, "You've been a big help. I couldn't have done it without you.

I don't think she got my sarcasm.

Padilla's eyes were bloodshot and he looked tired, as if he needed to sleep for about three days. It's hard being an emergency room doctor anywhere. He was a small man with long gray hair that was swept back from his forehead and curling in the back. He wore a white hospital coat and had glasses hanging from a cord around his neck.

"Mister Creakshrink?"

I nodded. We shook hands. I didn't bother to correct him. Under the circumstances, it wasn't important.

"Where's Dottie?" I asked.

"I must speak to you for a moment before you see her," he said.

He took my arm and led me to a worn couch against the wall. I looked around to orient myself. My best guess was that we were outside the intensive care unit. The hospital had the same scent all hospitals have, an uneasy combination of sickness and disinfectant.

"Please, sit down," he said.

Padilla sat next to me, threw one arm across the back of the couch, crossed his legs and turned in my direction.

"A truck driver found her naked at the side of the highway," he said. "Her car, no, her, ah, ..."

"SUV," I said.

He nodded. "Yes, thank you. Her SUV was hidden in the brush so that no one could see it from the road. She said that she was forced off the highway by two cars. She thinks there were three men, but only one of them assaulted her. When they forced her off the road, two men dragged her out of the car – excuse me, her SUV – and another man drove it deeper into the brush. At some point she was knocked unconscious and doesn't remember everything about the assault, which is a merciful thing. When she regained consciousness the men were gone and she managed to crawl up to the road where the truck driver found her and brought her here. That she was able to crawl so far in her condition is quite remarkable."

Padilla sank back into the couch, sighed, closed his eyes and ran the fingers of both hands through his hair. He gathered himself and picked up where he left off.

"As I said, she recalls being assaulted by only one man. Whoever did this must be very strong. She has a fractured skull. Her nose, cheekbone and jaw are broken, too. She has a broken arm and two broken ribs, plus many contusions and abrasions. If there is good news in any of this it is that barring complications I expect her to fully recover, at least physically. If any plastic surgery is needed, it should be minor, and probably won't be necessary. I cannot speak to the psychological effect. That is not my field. But she seems to be a very strong woman."

"Yes, she is," I said. "Doctor, was she, you know …?"

Padilla shook his head. "No, she was not sexually assaulted. However, there were traces of ejaculation on her body.'

I thought about that for a moment. I could feel the pressure build up inside my head. My hands balled into fists and I had to force myself to concentrate.

"Do you mean to say that whoever did this got off while he did it?" I asked. "That maybe he got off *because* he was doing it?"

"It's difficult to be sure, but assuming only one man was involved I would have to say yes," he explained. "Judging by her injuries and her description of what she remembered the man straddled her while he beat her. The ejaculation was found on her stomach and breasts."

"Do the police know?"

"Of course," he said. "We are required by law to make a report. An officer came here, I told him what she told me but I could not allow him to talk to her. I promised to call when she is capable of making a complete and thorough statement, which won't be for two or three days at least. The officer did speak to the truck driver, but I don't believe he had anything to add except that he found her on the road. By now, I assume that the police have found her clothes and her vehicle."

Padilla put his hands flat and pushed himself up from the couch as if it required some effort.

"You may have three minutes with her and not a second more," he said. "Do you understand?"

I nodded. Padilla led me down another hallway and

stopped in front of a room on the left. He put a hand on my shoulder and whispered in my ear: "Remember, three minutes."

The door was open. I quietly edged up to the bed. I could only see one eye and part of her left cheek and mouth. Everything else was either bandaged or covered. Her right arm was in an inflatable cast and held above her body by some hospital contraption. There was a chair at the foot of the bed. I quietly moved it to her side.

Her good eye opened and her mouth twitched. It might have been an attempt at a smile. It was hard to tell.

"Well if it isn't Mike Hammer," she said. Her voice was so low I could barely hear it.

"Sorry, but after midnight I turned into Sam Spade," I said. "Dottie, I know what happened. The doctor told me. You don't have to go over it all again. We don't have much time."

"Come closer."

I moved closer so that my head was next to hers.

"This has something to do with what you're working on, doesn't it?" The way she put it wasn't a question.

"Yes, I'm sure it does," I said. "I'm sorry I got you into this."

She didn't say anything. Her breathing was slow and regular. I sat back in my chair. She said something else but I couldn't quite hear it.

I leaned forward again. "What is it?"

"There was one man, a big man," she said. "He's the one who did it. The others just watched, I think. I never got a good look at them. He was huge, but all I remember is dark hair and eyebrows. He had a hard on. I could feel it when he got on top of me. He beat me with one hand and jerked off with another. I wanted you to know before the police."

I gently kissed her on the cheek and rose to leave.

"Wait!" Her voice was louder this time. The fingers of her good arm made a clutching motion.

"What is it, Dottie?"

"I want you to get the bastard," she said. "Promise me."

I got down on one knee and looked into her one good eye.

"Dottie, I promise."

CHAPTER 30

I LEFT Dottie's room and said goodbye to Doctor Padilla, who promised to call if there were any unexpected problems. I walked out to my car and stood for a moment with my arms on the roof, my eyes shut, and my forehead lowered against the cool metal.

After a few minutes, I drove back to the hotel, slowly this time. The bile rose in my throat and I had to swallow hard to keep it down. I wanted to strike out at something or someone, but there was nothing there. I took deep breaths to try to settle down but it didn't help. Without warning, I began to scream and beat on the steering wheel with my fists. By the time I got back to the hotel my voice was breaking from the strain.

Back in my room, I opened the sliding doors and walked out onto the balcony. The lights were off all over the complex. It was dark, I was alone, and I liked it that way. The moon was a thin sliver in the sky. Just like my first night here, there were so many stars it was as if a giant hand had flung them across the sky, the way I'd casually toss a handful of sand. I could see tiny lights far out on the ocean, probably ships rounding the peninsula and heading up the Sea of Cortez. Maybe one of them was a cruise ship, full of people having a good time? I didn't like the idea of people having a good time. Right now nobody should be having a good time. I could hear the gentle rhythm of the waves crashing on the beach. I usually found the sound to be soothing, but not tonight.

CHAPTER 31

It was a little after seven when my telephone rang. I was in bed drinking coffee. I hadn't slept at all since I got back from the hospital.

"Hello?"

"Ethan Cruickshank?"

"Yes."

"This is Andy Rosa."

If I'd been standing up I think I would have been necessary to sit down.

"Yes," I said.

"I think it's about time we met," he said.

"Maybe it is," I agreed. I hoped that I didn't sound as surprised as I was. "What do you have in mind?"

"We meet at some mutually acceptable place," he said. "I don't know what you're after, but maybe we can find a way to work things out."

"Where would this meeting be?" I asked.

"I'm open for suggestions as long as it's a safe place where you can't try anything cute," he said.

"And where you can't either," I said. "It cuts both ways."

"I'm not the one looking for you and I'm not the one who papered the town with flyers," he said. "You didn't show up for the meeting at the plaza and I don't blame you. It probably looked like a setup. I didn't have anything to do with it. I've been out of town and just learned about all this."

"What about the guy in my room?" I asked. "He wasn't exactly room service."

"That wasn't my idea either,' he said. "If I'd been here I wouldn't have done anything and you wouldn't know if I was within a thousand miles. In short, you'd have bubkus, pal."

"I suppose that what happened last night wasn't your idea either," I said.

I was surprised at how calm I felt. Maybe I'd used my anger up overnight? I felt a little light headed, as if I was removed from myself somehow. It was a familiar feeling. A dangerous one, too. I had to be careful or I might lose it again.

"Some of my people can be kind of hard to control, especially when they feel threatened," he said. "They over-reacted. It wasn't me."

I didn't believe him, but it didn't cost anything to keep the conversation going.

"So where do you think we might have this little chat of ours?"

Rosa thought about it, or seemed to.

"Can you handle a jet ski?" he asked.

"Yeah."

"How about we meet out in the middle of the bay? We can both see everything around us for a long way off, so there won't be any surprises."

"Just you and me?" I asked.

"Just you and me."

It was time to take the initiative.

"Okay," I said. "This morning at eleven."

He didn't hesitate. "I'll be there."

It was an irresistible offer. And he knew it.

CHAPTER 32

I DECIDED NOT to tell Suarez about the meeting. He'd want to come along, or at least be somewhere nearby, and I didn't want to take the chance of spooking Rosa.

Based on what he said, he probably intended to buy me off. From his point of view, there was no problem money couldn't solve. He had no reason to believe otherwise because it had been that way his whole life. He'd pay whatever it took, I'd go away, and he'd live happily ever after. What happened to Dottie was a warning of how it could go if I turned him down. Despite his denial, I had no doubt that he was behind it.

Without thinking about it, I realized that the beginning of a plan had bubbled up from my subconscious. It needed work, but it was a start. I sat on my balcony, drank coffee and listened to the waves while I refined it and shaped it. The fact that Rosa assumed that he could buy his way out of anything might work in my favor.

I felt more confident than at anytime since I started this case. Why was that? There was no reason for it because what happened to Dottie was my fault. Maybe this was the way the anger was coming out? Whatever the reason, I liked the feeling. It would help when I met

Rosa. If I felt that I was outwitting him it would make it easier to resist the urge to break his head open.

I rented the jet ski from a place on the *Playa Medano*, one of several beach operations that rented jet skis, snorkeling gear, kayaks, and offered hang gliding tours where the glider was tethered to a boat that zipped back and forth across the bay. Dina had gone up a couple of times. Not liking heights, I was happy to watch from the boat.

Rosa's promise that he'd be alone meant nothing, although it didn't seem likely that the brontosaurus would be part of it. I couldn't imagine that monster on a jet ski. He'd probably either sink it or slow it down so much that he might as well be riding a rock. As insurance, I had my Smith & Wesson in a holster under my shirt at the small of my back. Neither one of us said anything about being unarmed.

After checking out the bay and shoreline with binoculars and not seeing anything that scared me to death, I hopped on the jet ski and left the beach at ten fifty five. It was a calm day with a few fluffy clouds in the startling blue sky. I rode at less than half speed, my eyes moving back and forth across the water as I looked for anything that looked suspicious. Jet skis were popular in Cabo and there were already a half-dozen of them on the bay going nowhere in particular. This afternoon when it got warmer there'd probably be twice that many.

One of the cruise ships that travel the Mexican Riviera circuit of Acapulco, Puerto Vallarta, Mazatlan and Cabo had come in overnight. The big white "Love Boat" style ship was anchored not far from where we were supposed to meet. Water taxis were busy running passengers to the dock where they'd spend the day taking shore excursions and spending money. The ship loomed huge as I closed in on it, taller than a twenty-five story building.

As I neared the middle of the bay I cut back on the

throttle and slowed to a crawl. There was another jet ski about a hundred yards away. It had stopped and its engine was idling. It had to be Rosa. As I got closer I saw that it was. I put the engine in neutral and coasted up beside him but facing the opposite direction.

We stared at each other, each taking the measure of the other. Rosa's head was newly shaved and seemed to glisten in the sunlight. He wore a New York Giants t-shirt and yellow swim trunks that came to his knees. If he was as keyed up as I was, he didn't show it. He didn't seem nervous, or even particularly concerned. I watched his arrogant eyes to see if he involuntarily looked around for the help that must be nearby, but his gaze held study.

He lifted his shirt so I could see the waistband of his trunks.

"See? I'm unarmed," he said. "I know your name and you know who I am so an introduction seems pointless, doesn't it?"

"You could say that," I agreed.

"So what is it that you want, pal?" he asked. "Why the hell are you bothering me? What have I ever done to you?"

"Maybe I'm a writer and I'd like to write your life story." I didn't like being called "pal" by this slug, but kept it out of my voice. "You're a famous man, or should I say an infamous man. It could be a helluva book, maybe even a best seller."

He'd have to be an idiot to believe me, although he was obliging enough to continue the charade.

"Pal, that's exactly what I don't need in my life," he said. "Whatever might have happened in California is in the past, not that I did anything wrong. I'm not the first person to be hassled just because I'm rich. I'm happy to be out of there. Now I'm just a businessman in Mexico and I don't need somebody like you making trouble."

"Trouble?" I said. "All I did was had out a few flyers."

"Look, pal, let's cut the bullshit. I know the writer story is a crock," he said. "I don't know if you're a cop, or what. But whatever you are you can't do anything down here. I'm clean and I'm free and I intend to stay that way."

He waited for a response. When he didn't get one it seemed to make him edgy.

"Is somebody paying you to hassle me?" he asked.

I didn't say anything.

"Whatever it is, whatever you're getting, I'll double it," he said. "How does that sound? Why not take the easy way out? Like I said, sometimes I can't control my people. I'm sorry about your girlfriend, but anything can happen. I mean, you can always go back home. But her ...."

He didn't have to finish. As I expected, the offer came with a threat. He assumed that I was from California and he knew that Dottie was local.

"We might be talking about a lot of money," I said.

"I can afford it," he said, the familiar Rosa smirk creeping across his face.

With the other jet skis, a few small boats, and the water taxis moving tourists from the cruise ship to shore, *Bahia de Cabo San Lucas* was surprisingly noisy, a hum of indistinct sound that never went away. Sound carried over water, but it had an odd muting effect, too. As we talked, it was hard to pick out individual sounds to tell how near or far they were. I sensed that someone was in back of me and the urge to look was almost irresistible. But at the same time I didn't want to take my eyes off Rosa. He said he wasn't armed but I didn't believe him. After all, I was.

"So what about it?" he asked. "I'll pay you double

what you're getting and I'll take your word for how much. What could be fairer than that?"

"If I say yes, how will you handle it?".

"I'll have a cashier's check delivered to the hotel within ninety minutes after we leave here. Then you go home on the first flight you can get. I'll have somebody watching to make sure."

I stared at him as if I was thinking it over. The water lapped against the side of our jet skis. We'd drifted a little while we were talking so that the nose of my jet ski was pointed at Rosa on a ninety degree angle. I was tempted to draw my gun and take him right there, but if he had backup nearby I'd never get away with it.

"Okay, it's a deal," I said. "I get paid, I go away, and you leave Dottie alone. Right?"

"That's it," he said with a wide grin. "Like I said, you'll have you're check within ninety minutes. How much?"

I told him and his grin got even wider.

"Pal, congratulations on a very lucrative trip to Mexico," he said. "It was a pleasure doing business with you. When you leave, ignore the two guys in back of you. They were insurance in case you did something dumb."

"Yeah, I know. But they're too far back for a good shot. If *they* tried anything dumb you'd have been the first to go down. Pal, you need a better class of help."

I turned away and accelerated hard, driving my jet ski between the twins waiting on their jet skis about forty yards away. One of them waved as I roared past.

CHAPTER 33

MY MESSAGE LIGHT was blinking when I got back to my room. It was Suarez. Instead of calling back, I started calling the airlines to find two tickets to Los Angeles. It wasn't easy on short notice. I finally found two seats on a Mexicana flight in the early evening.

I called Suarez.

"Get packed," I said. "We're leaving."

"What?"

"We're leaving." I told him the flight time. "Do something with your gun. Hide it someplace where you're sure that no one will find it, but where you can recover it pretty quickly. I'll meet you in the lobby two hours before the flight. I'll explain later."

When I finished with Suarez, I got my gun and the boxes of shells, put the gun in my waistband, put the boxes in my pockets, grabbed a couple of hotel towels and walked out to the beach.

The beach was slightly curving. I walked far enough to be sure that I wasn't being followed and that I couldn't be seen from the hotel. If someone was watching me, and there certainly was, they were watching to make sure that I left Cabo San Lucas, not to eyeball my last walk on the beach. Using an unusually tall wind-bent palm tree as my bearing, I sat down like I was contemplating the ocean and used one hand to wrap the gun and boxes of shells in the towels and bury them in the sand. With the palm tree I could find them easily enough. Just like buried treasure.

When I got back to my room the message light was blinking again. I called the desk and was told that a messenger had an envelope for me and needed my signature. I walked down to the desk and signed. It was my check, as promised, a helluva lot of money.

I returned to my room, took a shower and packed. With me leading, our little two-car caravan drove to the Hertz office near the airport in San Jose. We returned the cars and the Hertz shuttle took us to the airport.

Suarez was dying to know what was going on, but I told him I'd explain when we were in the air. What happened to Dottie made me as cautious as I probably should have been all along.

As the jet lifted off, I turned to Suarez. He was in the window seat. I had the aisle.

"Dottie was beaten up after she left us last night," I said. "They forced her off the road on her way home."

Suarez's eyes narrowed. "How is she?"

I told him everything that Doctor Padilla told me, and about my brief conversation with Dottie. I also told him about my jet ski adventure out on the bay. Suarez's handsome young face hardened until it looked like a skull only thinly covered with flesh.

"Considering what you had me do with my gun I'd say we're not running away," he said. "You just want to look like it."

"Something like that," I said. "We can't hassle with our guns at customs and there wasn't time to get Espada here. Rosa's people know me. In case they've made you, too, both of us had to leave. I should have been more careful from the beginning."

"Maybe careful didn't have anything to do with what happened to Dottie," he said. "Maybe it was just bad luck. It could have been anything. Somebody could have seen us at the restaurant last night."

"Maybe," I agreed.

"Or maybe somebody saw us on the street after," he said. "There's nothing you could have done. Don't be so hard on yourself. What matters is what we do now."

Suarez sat back in his seat. His fingers drummed on the arm. The flight attendant pushed the drink cart up the aisle. We told her we didn't want anything.

"You want Rosa to think he's won," Suarez said. "We'll stay away for a little while, probably not too long. Then we'll come back and finish the job."

"You're damn right we will," I said.

"That's what I wanted to hear," he said. "Why don't you try to get some sleep? You look like hell."

"Okay, I'll give it a shot," I agreed. "If I'm lucky, the next sound you hear will be my snoring."

It probably wasn't the next sound, but it was close. I didn't wake up until we started the long descent into Los Angeles.

Still yawning from my nap, while we stood in line for the immigration check, I asked Suarez, "By the way, where'd you hide your gun?"

"I wrapped it inside a big baggie," he said. "Then I put it under my shirt, walked out on the beach and sat down like I was contemplating nature. I dug a hole with my left hand, the one away from the hotel so nobody could see, and left it there."

"Yeah, that's pretty much what I did, too," I said, "only I used hotel towels."

"Ethan," he said, "I want that brontosaurus bastard."

"Me, too," I said.

CHAPTER 34

WE GAINED an hour between Los Cabos and Los Angeles, so it wasn't that late by the time we got off the plane, made our way through the long and winding line to get back into the country, and snagged our luggage off the carousel.

Bags in hand, we walked out of the international terminal, caught the shuttle to the Hertz office and rented cars for each of us. While I fiddled with the paperwork for the cars, Suarez got on his cell phone and made reservations for us to fly back to Cabo in two days. We agreed to meet at the gate ninety minutes before departure.

He still had my digital camera. I asked him if he'd e-mail the photos of Rosa, the brontosaurus, and the girl to Chango.

"Tell Chango I'll call him," I said. "I want to try to find out who the big guy is."

"Why don't you send 'em?" he asked. "I mean, it's your camera anyway."

"I don't know how," I admitted.

Suarez grinned. "I see. Progress ...."

"... has passed me by again," I said.

"Okay, I'll take care of it," he said. "See you in a couple of days."

The drive north to the Marriott in Oxnard took about two hours. On the way I called Heenan on his cell phone number. It took three tries before I got through.

"Where the hell are you?" he asked indignantly. "They told me you checked out."

"We did," I said. "We're back in California."

"Let me see if I understand," he grumbled. "You know I'm coming down here so you go back there and now I'm the only one down here."

"That's pretty much it," I said. "But you can relax. We'll be back in a couple of days. I'll explain everything then. In the meantime, keep a low profile, if that's possible for you. Don't do anything to call attention to yourself and don't go asking around about Rosa. Act like a tourist and go fishing or something. I'll contact you when we get in."

"Do my ears deceive me?" he said. "It actually sounds like you've got a plan."

"You might say that," I said. "By the way, I take it you that didn't have any trouble getting into the country?"

"Not a bit," he said. "I used my real passport, too."

"Maybe you're not as wanted as you think you are?"

"A lot of people tell me that," he said. "And maybe Mexico's still a little sloppy in the realm of security. Whatever. I'll see you in a couple of days."

I called Chango. He wasn't at headquarters, but I caught him at home.

"Did you talk to your son?" I asked.

"He left a message," he said. "We haven't talked yet."

"Did he e-mail you the photographs?"

"He said he did. I haven't had a chance to look."

"Can pay special attention to one of the guys in the

pictures, the big one who looks like a thundercloud?" I asked.

"Oh, hell yes," he said. "I don't have anything else to do. Always happy to be of service to anyone who calls. You have a name? Names are kind of a help."

"Sarcasm noted," I said. "I don't have a name but it'll probably be a lot easier than you think. This guy stands out, I mean, he *really* stands out. There's nobody else on planet earth who looks like him. You'll understand when you see the pictures."

I explained that he was working for Rosa and I wanted to know who we were dealing with. I didn't tell him about Dottie. Somehow it would have seemed like a violation of her privacy.

"Okay, I'll give it a shot," he said. "I'll let you know if I find anything."

I called the hospital in Cabo San Lucas. After being put on hold a half-dozen times I finally reached Doctor Padilla.

He said that Dottie couldn't talk. "She is sleeping and that's the best thing for her."

"How is she?" I asked.

"As expected," he said. "If there are no complications, it should be as I told you."

"Thanks, doctor," I said. "I'll be calling you again."

"There was a police officer asking about you," he said. "A lieutenant."

" Valencia?" I asked. "A young good looking guy?"

"Yes, that's the one," he said. "I allowed him to speak with Miss Winthrop for a brief time. I believe she told him that she had dinner with you before ... the incident. He would very much like to talk to you. He was very forceful."

"Yeah, I bet he was," I said. "I'll call him. Thank you again, Doctor."

I called the number on the card that Donald Taft gave me.

"Hello."

The voice was male and vaguely accented, but it could have been an accent from anywhere.

"Donald Taft, please."

"Who may I say is calling?"

"Tell him it's Ethan Cruickshank."

In a minute or so, I heard Taft's voice.

"This is Taft."

"It's Ethan Cruickshank."

"Yes."

"I'd like to meet tomorrow."

"Where are you?"

"I'm at the Marriott in Oxnard," I explained. "It's just for a short time. I go back to Cabo in a couple of days."

"What are you doing here?" he asked.

" I'll explain everything when we meet," I said. "Sometime early in the morning, if that's possible."

"Be here at eight," he said.

"Thanks," I said. "I'll see you then."

CHAPTER 35

CHANGO CALLED me at the hotel late that night.

"Christ, Cruickshank, you sure can pick 'em," he said.

"Chango, an explanation might help," I asked.

"Okay, I tapped a couple of guys I know at the DEA and the more I found out the worse it got," he said. "The big boy is named Hector Macias. A few years back, he was the big he-bull on Mexico's national weightlifting team. He was a sure thing for the Olympics until he peed the wrong way, got busted for steroids and thrown off the team. Macias dropped out of sight for a while and then showed up working as muscle for the Mexican drug assholes. He's never been charged for anything but he's suspected in the killing of at least seven men and two women. What makes Macias different is that he beats them to death with his bare hands. He's scary enough that sometimes just the threat of this guy gets the job done. The DEA guy says he's a sicko who gets off on it."

"You mean, he really gets off," I asked. "That's not just a figure of speech."

"Yeah," he said. "Really."

"That fits with what happened to somebody I know down there," I said.

"I know what happened to the woman," Chango said. "I had a talk with Tony."

"So Rosa hired this character to keep people like us off his back or scare us away," I said.

"It's not that simple," he said. "It gets worse, too. Eventually Macias wound up working for a guy named Raul Castrillon, a Cuban who moved to Mexico, spent some time in La Palma, Mexico's principal maximum security prison, and put together an ambitious operation of his own when he got out. He was a young arrogant bastard who tried to get control of at least one of Mexico's principal drug routes. He went after one cartel that controlled the eastern border crossings with Texas in the state of Tamaulipas. When that didn't work he went after another one that controlled the western border between Tijuana and El Paso. He damn near pulled that one off. The rival leaders eventually formed an alliance to get Castrillon. They wound up blowing him and his private jet out of the sky just after take off from Tijuana. They probably used a Stinger missile. You know the Stinger, right? It's an American-made, shoulder-fired ground-to-air missile. The missile and launcher only weigh about thirty pounds and it's deadly to any aircraft within four miles of its launch point. It's ...."

"I get the picture," I had to stop Chango before he got too carried away. He loved that kind of stuff. "What does all this have to do with us?"

"Castrillon's wife took over after her husband's death," he continued. "She's a nasty piece of work, maybe even worse than her husband. They call her '*La Puerca.*'"

"The Pig?" I asked. "Is that a commentary on her looks?"

"Not at all," Chango explained. "She's supposed to be a hell of a good looking woman, although as far as I know nobody really knows what she looks like. There aren't any photographs of her, only descriptions. The name has to do with her appetites, everything from sex to power. She killed the men who killed her husband and then she killed their families. She didn't do it personally, but her people did. That led to an out-and-out war that drained everybody's resources and manpower, but especially hers since practically everybody else was aligned against her. At least forty people have been killed so far. The thing is, Macias is like a big dog who's devoted to *La Puerca* and doesn't do anything without orders from her. If he's with Rosa it's because she wants him there. He's sure as hell not there for the conversation. Among his other charms, he's what you might call stupid. His knuckles probably drag on the ground when he walks."

"Almost," I said. "Thanks, Chango."

"Cruickshank, understand me, there's more going on here than you thought," he warned. "You better be damn careful. Tony's a big boy who can take care of himself, but if anything happens to him, your problem won't be with me, it'll be with his mother. Believe me, you'd rather have me on your case than her."

"Thanks for caring," I said.

"I don't give a fuck about you," he said. "It's my son I'm worried about."

I put the telephone back in its cradle with Chango's warm words still ringing in my ears.

CHAPTER 36

I CALLED Dina at six thirty the next morning, which left me plenty of time to get to Taft's place by eight. She answered the telephone again. It was in the middle of the afternoon at *Villefranche de Conflent* and she said her Dad was taking a nap.

Except for my conversation with Chango last night, I told her everything that happened, right from the beginning. I'd already told her a lot of it, but for context it was better to start at the beginning. I didn't tell her what Chango told me because I didn't know what it meant, although after sleeping on it I was pretty sure that I knew who did.

At the end, I told her I was going back to finish the job.

The silence lasted for what seemed like five minutes, but probably wasn't that many seconds.

"I am not wild about the idea, but after everything you've told me I know that you have to finish it yourself, or at least you think you have to," she said.

"Especially after what happened to Dottie," I said. "What Rosa did up here was bad enough, and I'd want to

see it through to the end anyway, but there was a particular viciousness about what they did to her."

"So tell me, husband of mine, exactly when did you
become Captain Marvel, savior of the universe?" she
asked pointedly.

In my minds' eye, I could see her head tilted to one
side and her dark and shining eyes coming at me with
the question. We'd been married for so long there were
times when I couldn't remember what life was like
without her. I'd caused her a lot of grief over the years.
Through it all, Dina had more patience and showed more
love than I deserved or had any right to expect. I was
never able to completely shake the feeling that she was
better for me than I was for her and it made me feel
guilty sometimes.

"Kid, I know what you mean and you have every
right to ask," I said. "But it's what I was hired to do. If I
don't see it through, then why am I doing this? But more
than that, everything that's happened since I started on
this makes it important that I finish the job. I mean, we
could always stop and try to work it out through the
Mexican government, but we'd still face the same
problem we had when we started and Rosa'd probably
get away, go someplace else and start all over again."

"Besides, it's personal now, isn't it?" she said. "What
happened to your friend Dottie made it that way."

"Yeah, it did," I agreed. "Suarez feels the same way. If
I dropped out he'd go it alone and I can't let that happen.
It's too much for one man to handle by himself."

So there it was and there wasn't anything either one
of us could do about it.

"I do have some good news," I said.

"What?"

"Big Eddie's joined us. He's in Cabo already. That's
worth something."

"Yes, that's worth something," she agreed. "A very considerable something, I'd say."

Being separated by so much distance didn't feel right. It was as if the thousands of miles between us somehow made it harder to talk to each other, to say what we felt. Even so, when it was time to say goodbye neither of us wanted to let go.

"Ethan, there's something else you haven't mentioned," she said.

"What's that?" I asked, worried that she'd somehow guessed that there was more to it than what I'd told her.

"That man Rosa cannot be allowed to live free in our home," she said. "Neither one of us could stand knowing he was there, not for one second."

It seems strange, but in all this time that had never occurred to me.

And, of course, she was right.

CHAPTER 37

DESPITE WHAT HE'D said about only coming out to the patio at dusk to watch the animals at the lake, it was as if Taft hadn't moved since the first time I saw him.

Only the time of day was different. It was early enough that there was still a chill in the air. The crisp morning light made the lake seem brighter and newer. Taft wore the same deck shoes that I remembered; the khaki's with the knife-edge crease, too. Instead of a blue long-sleeved shirt with epaulets, he wore a green long-sleeved sweater to ward off the chill. The salt-and-pepper beard was shaggier, as if he hadn't trimmed it since I saw him last.

Boyer was there, too. I'd hoped that he wouldn't be, but knew that he probably would. He was his usual elegant self in a cream suit with a light-blue show handkerchief in the jacket pocket, a matching shirt, a red silk tie, and outrageously expensive Italian loafers. He didn't seem that pleased to see me. The feeling was mutual.

Compared to Boyer, in my Wrangler jeans, black loafers, and a navy blazer over a white polo shirt, I was underdressed, but I wasn't hired for my sartorial splendor.

I was escorted to the patio by a young Latino male dressed in black pants and a white jacket. Taft was on the telephone again, barking out orders. I read once that the more powerful a person is the less clutter there is on their desk. Apparently Taft was so powerful that he didn't even need a desk. He didn't bother to get up. He just waved me to the same chair I had at our first meeting. Boyer took a position that faced us and blocked the view. With his backside on the slate wall that ringed the patio and his legs crossed at the ankles, he was the very picture of lawyerly insouciance; casual but oh so attentive.

Taft finished his conversation and put the telephone on the table beside him.

"Coffee?" he asked.

"Don't do it just for me," I said. "But if you're having some, then I will."

"Do you want some or not?"

All I could do was laugh. Only Taft could turn coffee into a confrontation.

"Sure," I said. "Why not?"

Taft stared at Boyer, who resisted as long as he could before he scurried off. Assuming that Boyer was on the clock, it may have been the most expensive coffee fetch in history.

"I hope that you actually have something to tell me and you're not here to waste my time," Taft said.

"Did anybody ever tell you that you have the personality of a snake?" I asked.

Instead of getting angry, Taft seemed amused.

"Congratulations," he said. "Not many have the nerve to say it to my face."

"Lucky me," I said. "Should we wait until Boyer gets back, or do you want to start without him?"

Taft ignored my question and went off on his own track.

"You know, Cruickshank, down the road I might have uses for a man like you," he said. "If you're successful, once this is over how would you like to work for me?"

"That's a big 'if'," I said. "Besides, you don't know if you'd like me working for you and I sure as hell doubt that I'd like working for you, whatever I'd be doing. And don't forget, I don't even live in this country anymore."

Taft made a little waving motion with his hand to indicate that the subject was dropped, for now.

Boyer returned. Concern that he might have missed something was etched all over his face. A moment later, the coffee arrived. It was delivered by the same young Latino who led me to the patio. He set the silver tray on the table between us. He poured some for Taft and some for me. Boyer declined. He probably thought the color of the coffee cup clashed with his suit.

"Why don't you get started?" Taft said.

As I did with Dina last night, I started at the beginning. Boyer had already heard some of it. Presumably he'd passed it on to Taft, but I didn't know that for sure. I also wanted Taft to hear it from me because I didn't know what kind of spin Boyer might have put on it.

I went though everything in detail. When I came to the part about Dottie Winthrop being assaulted, Boyer winced, but Taft's expression never changed. For all he cared, I might as well have told him that she received a vigorous scolding. I finished with my conversation with Chango last night.

"I've got to hand it to you, Cruickshank, that's quite a story." Boyer was in a tough-guy mode that I hadn't seen before. If it hadn't seemed so silly it might have been offensive. "Don't tell me that suddenly it's all too difficult and you're quitting."

Taft made a motion with his hand, which I interpreted

as a signal for Boyer to shut up. Apparently Boyer did, too.

"Cruickshank already told me he's going back to Cabo San Lucas, and not just because he lives there," he said. "I assume that's still the case."

I nodded. "I've got a flight tomorrow. Suarez is going back, too, but we're doing this on one condition."

It occurred to me that Taft had let on more than he may have intended. As he said, I'd already told him I was going back. It was interesting that he hadn't bothered to tell Boyer. Maybe Boyer wasn't as necessary to Taft as Boyer thought he was? Now *there* was an encouraging thought.

"It's a little late for conditions, isn't it?" Taft asked.

"There's more going on that any of us thought and I think you know what it is," I said. "I had doubts about your story in the first place but I let Heenan talk me into it. He doesn't care if you're the anti-christ as long as your check clears. But after everything that's happened, plus what Chango told me, now I'm sure your story's bullshit. I'll call the whole thing off right now unless you tell me the truth. What's your interest in this thing, your *real* interest?"

I was taking a risk. Suarez was going back no matter what. If he went, I'd have to go, too. But Taft didn't know that.

Boyer couldn't take it anymore. He looked like his ears were about to blow off the side of his head.

"Mister Taft, I don't know what Cruickshank is talking about but I most strongly advise against letting this idiotic scheme go any further."

This time he was speaking in his best courtroom voice. I almost expected him to cry, "I object." If I cared about his opinion, I might have turned cranky at the emphasis he put on "idiotic." He hit "scheme" pretty hard, too.

Boyer pushed himself off the wall and started pacing back and forth. I couldn't tell if he was genuinely opposed, reacting this way because he didn't like me, trying to impress Taft, or all three.

"If you'll recall, I was against this project from the first and nothing that's happened makes me like it any better," he said. "This so-called plan of Cruickshank's seems very dicey to me. If all this ... this *buccaneering* doesn't work, everyone could wind up in a Mexican jail, everyone except Rosa, a man who has committed no crime in Mexico and will likely be seen as the aggrieved party. After all, it will be our agents who're breaking the law, not him. Something else to consider is that sooner or later it will get out that you're involved and that could have a detrimental effect on your business interests in Mexico. Believe me ...."

"Roger, shut up!"

The words were hard but it was the tone that hurt most. Boyer stopped pacing and jerked himself erect. He'd been hit smack in his big fat ego, embarrassed by Taft's order to shut his yap, and doubly embarrassed that I was there to hear it. I tried not to smile. I just didn't try very hard.

Boyer didn't go down easy. I'll give him that.

"Mister Taft, you pay me to advise ...."

"I pay you to do what I tell you to do!" Taft put his hands on the arms of the chair, as if he might jump to his feet and punch Boyer in the snoot.

Boyer reacted as if he'd been slapped in the face; he recoiled, stepped back and bumped into the wall he'd been lounging against so confidently a few minutes earlier.

"Sir, I object to ..."

"I don't give a damn what you object to," snarled Taft. "Cruickshank and I have some private matters to discuss. Go away! Now!"

Boyer's mouth opened and closed, but nothing came out. It may have been the first time in his life that words failed him. He probably had other clients, but Donald Taft was *the* client. Roger Boyer had just been thrown off the mother ship. It was only temporary, but it hurt.

Boyer looked at Taft. He looked at me. He looked back at Taft. Nobody offered a reprieve or said, "April Fool!" Head down, he gingerly stepped around us and trudged toward the house. It must have been the longest and most humiliating walk of his life.

"I see that you're an understanding boss," I said.

Taft smiled, his teeth flashing white against his beard.

"Roger doesn't know as much about my activities as he thinks he does," Taft explained. "In fact, there are many things he doesn't know at all, although I'm sure he has his suspicions. He has his uses, but he's also the kind of man who needs to be taken down a peg or two from time to time."

Since I didn't like Boyer, I didn't see anything wrong with taking him down a peg or ten.

"So you want to know what's going on?" he asked. "Given what you've found out, I don't blame you."

Taft inhaled and seemed to gather himself like a man about to jump off the high dive.

"Rosa has become quite friendly with the woman known as *La Puerca*," he said. "We don't know how they first came in contact, but we got on to it when he was seen coming from her complex near Guadalajara. Thanks to a DEA agent who was subsequently killed, we know that Rosa agreed to become her partner. Your friend Suarez has excellent sources. Her resources are stretched very thin and Rosa's money – his fortune is closer to one hundred million dollars than the usually reported fifty - will not only revitalize her operation, it could make it supreme in Mexico, especially since the recent offensive by the Mexican government either killed or jailed several of the other cartel leaders."

Taft rubbed the side of his beard.

"In short, there's a vacuum at the top and she wants to fill it. We'd rather she didn't."

I poured myself another cup of coffee. It wasn't as chilly as it was when I arrived, but I felt awfully cold inside.

"But ultimately what does it matter?" I asked. "We're losing the so-called war on drugs anyway. As long as it's run with the same bungling that fills our prisons with bottom-feeding users and dealers and leaves the big boys untouched, who cares who the top dog in Mexico is since there's always going to be a top dog?"

"Your point is well taken, although we've actually made more progress than you think," Taft admitted. "As I said, Mexico's had some success in creating this vacuum we're talking about. However, we're particularly concerned about the Castrillon woman's plan for the New Mexico border."

Taft paused to see if I had any questions.

"Go on," I said.

"Despite the stories you read, the most popular and reliable way to get drugs across the border still involves muling it over," he said. "These mules, usually profes- sionals who do it repeatedly, mix with the illegals. They carry loads of marijuana, heroin or cocaine and cross the border by the thousands."

"I know all that," I said.

"I'm sure you do, but the context will help you under- stand the problem," Taft said. "For years, the preferred crossings were in Texas and Southern California because they were closer to major cities and transportation centers. Tightened security there funneled much of that activity into Arizona, which is now the busiest illegal crossing point in the country. Hundreds of arrests were made last year, which means that many more than that got through. But Arizona has beefed up its defenses. Not enough, but better that they were. More than two thousand agents patrol that border, supported by manned and unmanned surveillance aircraft and a lot of other sophisticated technology."

I drained the last of my coffee and put the cup back in its saucer.

"With Rosa's money, the Castrillon woman wants to establish a major route at the New Mexico border," Taft continued. "Palomas, which is just across the border from Columbus, New Mexico, would probably be her hub to move people and drugs into this country. Deming, not far north of Columbus, is her likely distribution point, although there will undoubtedly be more than one. From her perspective, it's a fantastic opportunity. There are a little more than four hundred agents to patrol more than fourteen thousand square miles of empty territory. Most of the border is unmarked and open. There aren't even many fences, boundary lines, or roads to show which side is which. Since it is involved in drug traffic and illegal immigration everywhere else, there is no doubt that elements of the Mexican military will be involved, too. Drugs aside, the illegal immigration business is by itself remarkably lucrative. If one large operation can get one hundred thousand illegals over the border at five hundred dollars a head, that's fifty million dollars. The true rate is probably closer to a thousand dollars."

"I can't believe somebody else isn't already using the New Mexico border," I said.

"They are," replied Taft, "but not to the extent or with the sophistication *La Puerca* intends to bring to it."

"Why don't we just beef up the defenses the way we did in California and Arizona?"

"We will, but it takes money and time," he said. "It probably won't surprise you to hear than they can move faster than we can. Besides, it's better to stop a flood before it starts that to try to stop it once it's begun."

I shrugged at that. "Even if you win this one, someone else will come along."

"True, but this is what faces us now" Taft agreed. "We'll deal with the future when it comes."

"There's another element to this," he added. "As a result of his association with *La Puerca* Rosa has a great deal of valuable information that we would like to squeeze out of him. Obviously, we can only do that if he's in our possession, and that is where you came in. The reasons why we can't do anything officially are generally what you were told they are."

"So all that business about your daughter was just a way to get me hooked," I said. "It sounded as phony as it was."

"But it worked, didn't it?" he said.

If he'd smirked, I think I would have hit him in the mouth.

"It was the perfect way to appeal to you. We needed to be involved to have some element of control and to keep abreast of your activity. Heenan's involvement was sheer coincidence. It didn't matter one way or the other, except to give my offer some legitimacy in your eyes. I do have a daughter, and it's true that I haven't seen her in years, but as far as I know she lives in Philadelphia and never met Andy Rosa."

"Why didn't you tell me all this at the beginning?" I asked.

Taft took his time. It was as if he was a teacher trying to explain something to an exceptionally dull student.

"If I had come to you and said, 'Your government needs you,' what would you have said?" he asked.

"That it's not my government anymore," I admitted. "That the best thing to do is to legalize all these so-called controlled substances, which would immediately eliminate most of the multi-billion dollar profits. The stuff would be sold in licensed stores, with what profit there was going to rehab programs. The allure of doing something illegal would be gone and there'd be no point in gangs pushing the stuff in schools to find new customers. On the other hand, I might not have bothered with all that. I probably would have told you to go piss up a rope."

"Your patriotism is stirring and your solution is simplistic," he said.

"What's stirring right now is my nausea," I said. "And my solution is better than you've got. Right now you're just sticking your fingers in the holes in the dike and you're running out of fingers."

"But now you're in too deep to get out," he said. "You want to finish this job, don't you?"

I didn't answer right away, but I knew what the answer was. So did Taft.

"Yes, I do," I said. "But I'm going to tell everyone involved exactly what's going on. They deserve to know."

"Deserve?" Taft seemed puzzled, as if the concept was foreign to him. "If you must, I won't stop you."

"No," I said, "you won't."

There was silence between us. I was curious about exactly who Donald Taft was, but I didn't want to ask. Government? Private? Some mix of both? It didn't really matter. If I asked him, he'd probably just lie to me again.

My loathing rose from deep inside like vomit. I controlled it. I didn't like it, but I controlled it.

Taft watched while the emotions surged through me. I didn't try to hide it and the look on my face told him everything.

"You don't know who you dislike the most, me or Andy Rosa," he said.

"Something like that," I said.

"As long as the job gets done it doesn't really matter, does it?" he said.

Taft straightened in his chair. "Let's get down to business. As I see it, you want them to think that you've run so they'll let their guard down. Do I have that right?"

"Exactly," I said, putting my feelings for Taft aside. "If they're not looking for us, it'll be easier to surprise them."

"What will you do when you get back?" he asked.

"Eddie Heenan's down there now, so there will be three of us," I said. "I hope to recruit Valencia, too. His presence might give us some legal cover. Even if it doesn't, he'll be a good man to have on our side. But whether or not he joins us, we're going to hit the house and grab Rosa there."

"Why at the house?" Taft asked. "That only seems to make an already tricky situation even more difficult. Why not out on the street or in one of the clubs Rosa seems to like so much?"

"A club would be too crowded and there are too many ways to get away on the street," I explained. "At the same time, while I don't want to use guns when we do this, Rosa's people may not have the same reluctance. If we tried to grab Rosa in public and somebody starts shooting it would be easy for civilians to get hurt. In that case, the Mexican authorities would not love us, not that there's much chance they'll love us anyway. Rosa or his people may be armed when they go out, but chances are pretty good that they won't be carrying in the house."

"I still don't understand why you don't want to use your weapons," he said. "Maybe a few people you don't know might get hurt but ...."

He didn't say, "So what?" He didn't have to. He really didn't see why it mattered. Donald Taft was what he was, but finally he wasn't pretending to be anything else.

"Like I said, if both sides start blasting away anything could happen and I'm not sure that the Mexican police would see any difference between them and us," I said. "And remember the original goal; neither you nor Heenan want Rosa dead. When people start shooting, anybody can go down. I'm trying to do what you hired me to do. Either I'm running this operation or I'm not."

"What do you need from me," he said.

"Boyer was right about one thing," I said. "Things could get tricky when we make our move. In Mexico, you're guilty until proven innocent. Whether it works or whether it doesn't, we're going to need all the clout you've got."

"What do you want me to do?" he asked.

"I'll have your number on speed dial," I explained. "If we grab Rosa, the Mexicans will probably throw us all in jail while they sort it out. At that point, somebody's going to have to make sure that Rosa stays in custody so he can't run again. At the same time, I'd like to keep us from serving a long sentence in a Mexican jail. Eddie already has a history down there. This time they might bury him. The problem is that we won't be in a position to help ourselves and Rosa probably has legal help close at hand. We don't want them to move faster than we do."

"I understand," Taft said.

"I'll call you whether or not we're successful," I explained. "But either way I may not have any time to talk before they take my phone away, so just getting a call from me should tell you that we need your help unless I say otherwise. Speed will be very important."

"I'll contact Espada," Taft said. "He'll have a team ready and waiting in Cabo, with another in Mexico City. I'll do the same here. Call me just before you make your move so we'll have a sense of the timing."

""What about General Urrea?" I asked. "Can he help?'

"I don't know," Taft admitted. "Urrea has his own agenda. If it furthers his cause – which generally involves the accumulation of power and money, although money seems to be a secondary consideration – he may help. If not, he probably won't. I've never known him to be motivated by anything other than self interest."

"Kind of like you," I said.

Taft's eyes narrowed. We tried to stare each other down. Nobody won.

"Actually he's not at all like me," he said. "But I wouldn't expect you to understand."

"Maybe it has something to do with Valencia?" I suggested. "Urrea seems to think highly of him."

"His motives really don't matter," Taft said. "Come the time, I'll contact Urrea. We'll see what happens then, but it's not something you should count on."

He got to his feet, a sign that our cozy little get together was finished. Not wanting to be looked down on, I got up, too.

"Let me give you Espada's number," Taft said. "Call us both, if you can. I'll tell him that you may not be able to talk, so the call by itself should get him started. Unlike Roger, he isn't afraid to take the initiative."

"Good idea," I said. "I should have thought of that myself."

I decided that I wanted to know after all.

"One last question," I said.

"What is it?"

"Who the hell are you?" I asked.

"Does that really matter now?" he said.

He wasn't going to tell me and I decided not to press. I regretted asking at all. It looked weak.

I reached into my pocket, pulled out Rosa's cashier's check and handed it to Taft.

"Here," I said. "I don't want it."

CHAPTER 38

My NEXT STOP was to see my psychiatrist.

"So tell me, how did it go after we talked last time?" he asked.

In a very real sense, these therapy sessions were all about me. That wasn't selfish. That was their purpose. At least that's what I told myself. Consequently I put more emphasis on how I felt and what I thought, as opposed to the simple ABCs of what happened, although in this case the ABCs were anything but simple.

When I finished, he cradled his chin in one hand and asked the inevitable question: "How do you feel?"

His voice was soothing. It always was. A long time ago, I'd joked that they must teach it to psychiatry students. He replied that, yes, they do, more or less. Keeping the patient calm while the psychiatrist remained neutral was an important part of therapy, although he added that's not always the right way, or, as he put it, it's not always "appropriate." Sometimes in therapy you want the bottled up emotions to come flying out. But the ability to calm was a valuable skill for any psychiatrist.

"As usual, how I feel isn't simple and it's hard to describe," I said. "There's a lot of things all mixed together. I know that's not a very good description, but it's the best I can do. I'm eager and glad that I'm finally coming to the end of it, but on the other hand I can't *see* the end of it. There are too many possibilities. A lot of things could happen, some of them good, some of them not so good. I don't like the uncertainty, but it comes with the situation. There isn't anything I can do about it. I'm angry, mostly about what happened to Dottie, but I'm angry about being used, too. I want to get Hector as much as I want to get Rosa. Sometimes I find myself grinding my teeth and I didn't know I was doing it. That's a little scary. Taft was right when he talked about how I feel about him. In his way, he's almost as detestable as Rosa."

"As much as we don't like it, aren't people like Taft necessary in the world we live in?" he said.

"Maybe, but that doesn't mean I have to like it," I said.

As we sat in the semi-darkness of his office and talked about intimate things, I could feel tension flow out of me as if someone had pulled a plug. Until then, I didn't realize how pumped up I was. I suppose that I knew it in an intellectual way, but I didn't feel it the way I needed to really know it. As we talked, I felt like I was melting into the soft chair and becoming part of it. At the same time, there was a tingling on my scalp and my voice and my brain felt detached from the rest of me.

When I mentioned how peculiar I felt, as usual, he had an answer. And, as usual, it seemed obvious once he said it.

"You've been under an extraordinary strain and what you're feeling is a bit of relief," he said. "Your activities in Mexico were as stressful as anything could possibly be. You also feel a great deal of guilt about what happened to Dottie Winthrop. Too, with Dina gone dealing with each other by

telephone brought on a different kind of stress, with a reso-
lution that wasn't as satisfactory as it might have been face to
face. You knew that she would not be comfortable with what
you'd done and what was left to do. You probably dreaded
having to tell her about it. That doesn't mean you don't love
and trust her, but you've never been entirely comfortable
opening up to anyone. When you're pressed, it's too easy for
you to fall back on old habits. Your conversation this
morning was confrontational, too. You regard this office as a
safe place and you're letting your guard down. One of the
benefits of therapy is that in a way there's nothing at stake. I
don't think more or less of you at the end of a session."

"Okay, I get it," I said. "Now what?"

"For now, my advice is to try to stay in the moment,"
he said. "Don't dwell on what's already happened,
although that won't be easy. Focus on the task at hand.
The less baggage the better. This is not the time to try to
deal with the larger issues. You don't need distractions."

We talked for the rest of the hour. I was pretty sure
that it helped. A lot of the time I didn't know whether or
not a session helped until later and sometimes I wasn't
sure even then. It would be been nice to find the magic
bullet, but I never did. Maybe someday.

I knew that our time had run out, but he didn't say
anything.

"May I ask your advice about something," he said. "It
falls in your line of work."

"Of course," I said, surprised at the request.

"I have a patient, an ex-police officer I've been seeing
for years," he said. "Actually I have quite a few patients
in law enforcement."

"I'm not surprised," I said.

"At any rate, years ago, in another city, he was
assigned to protect someone, a woman whose ex-

husband had threatened her. Naturally he couldn't stay with her twenty fours hours a day, but he saw her home every night. He walked her to the door and waited outside until she was safe inside her house and turned on the lights. This went on for several weeks. One night he followed her home, as usual. He walked her to the door, she went inside, the light went on and he left. It turned out that her ex-husband was waiting inside and he killed her. My patient has been struggling with it ever since. He feels guilty, as if it was all his fault. We're making progress, but I'd like to know what you'd say to him if he was a friend of yours? As a friend and fellow professional, what would you tell him?"

"Nothing he doesn't already know," I said. "He just has to find a way to apply it to himself, and that's the hardest thing of all. You can never provide one hundred percent protection. It just isn't possible, especially for one man. From what you tell me, he did everything he could. No one can do more than that. Over time, the best you can hope for is to win more than you lose. If he was a good cop, he probably did. Sometimes there just isn't anything you can do."

A half-smile played on his lips. He looked a man who was proud of himself.

"Ethan, there's no such client," he admitted. "I was talking about you and Dottie Winthrop. I knew that you'd say what you did because it's right. What happened to her wasn't your fault. If it was someone you knew, you'd tell them that and you'd mean it. You don't have a family the way most other people do and you don't let many people get close. In a way, those few that do get close *are* your family, or at least substitute for it. For whatever reason, Dottie managed to get close in a very short time and that only adds to your guilt. Stop beating yourself up over it. No one can do more than what you're doing."

I should have seen it coming, but my mind was full of other things. The trick was so old that I couldn't believe I'd fallen for it. Was I really that dumb? Well, yes, sometimes I was. I felt like a blockhead for having been fooled so easily.

I fumbled for something to say.

"Dina's my family," I said. "Dina and Brewster."

"Yes they are, but you know very well what I mean."

"You know, down deep you're pretty damn tricky," I said.

"I know," he said. "Psychiatry will do that to you."

CHAPTER 39

I EXPLAINED the plan to Suarez on the flight down to Cabo.

"Feel free to argue and tell me if you think I'm missing something, but here's what I've come up with," I said. "I think our best chance is to grab Rosa at the house in Pedregal. They think we're gone so he should be feeling pretty safe, especially up there."

"Day or night?" he asked.

"Day. I don't want us blundering around in the dark. Too many things could go wrong."

Suarez tossed some airline peanuts in his mouth, chewed a while and washed it down with a Bohemia. With everything he did, his movements were so precise there was almost a kind of beauty to it.

"I know we're being paid to get Rosa, but what about the brontosaurus?" he asked. "You and I have a score to settle with that son of a bitch."

"I know, but let's take one thing at a time," I said. "Trust me, Tony, I haven't forgotten."

He nodded. "Okay. How do you want to hit the house? From the street, or from the beach?"

"If we can recruit Valencia, I want to go in both

ways," I explained. "He'll go to the front, ring the bell and announce himself. Unless he's alone, Rosa probably won't answer the door. He'll have somebody else do it. Valencia will ask to speak to Rosa. He'll be wearing civilian clothes but without saying so exactly he'll give the impression that he's there on official police business. The rest of us will come up the hill from the beach and be waiting. You remember from Dottie's photos how the pool was built out over the hill and the deck was supported by columns? If we can get that close without being seen, under the deck would be the perfect place to wait. We'll make our move once Valencia gets in and everybody's focused on him."

"Why have one in the front and three in back?" Suarez asked. "Why not give Valencia some support and make it two and two?"

"Rosa knows Eddie from back home," I explained. "They know me, too, so I can't go to the front door either. If they watched us leave Cabo then they've made you, too. Besides, I want you with us because you speak Spanish and we don't."

"You should learn, especially since you live in Mexico," Suarez said, gobbling down more peanuts.

"Yeah, I know," I said. "One of these days I will."

"Assuming we get Rosa, what do we do with him?" Suarez asked.

"That's another iffy part," I admitted. "The official line in Mexico is that we're supposed to contact the appropriate authorities, show a warrant from the States, inform them of the suspect's whereabouts and then let them make the arrest, which they might get around to eventually if they don't put it in a file and forget about it or call Rosa and warn him."

Suarez smiled. "I'd say we're not taking the official line."

"We can either hustle Rosa off to the Cabo police station and claim that Valencia made the arrest or drag him to the American Consul's office," I continued. "It's got to be one or the other. It's not like we can put Rosa in a steamer trunk and smuggle him out of the country. The consul's office is over by the marina. The faces would be a lot friendlier there and I think it's our best bet."

"Like you said, the whole thing sounds pretty tricky," Suarez agreed.

We sat in silence for a while. I wanted to give Suarez a chance to think things through. In the meantime, as usual, I was made drowsy by the hum of the engines and the vibration of the jet. The plane was packed with the usual crowd of Cabo revelers and there was an almost palpable sense of anticipation in the air. Good times, big fish, great golf and buckets of alcohol were just around the corner. Whoopee!

Suarez was so quiet I glanced over to see if he was still awake. His eyes were open and he was staring straight ahead.

"There's one other thing, Tony," I added. "I don't want anybody acting like a hero when we do this. I know you want the brontosaurus. Like I said, so do I. But don't get ambitious on your own. Judo won't do a hell of a lot of good against somebody that size."

He frowned and shook his head. "What judo?"

"Chango told me you've got a black belt," I said.

Suarez laughed so softly he might as well have been laughing to himself. I could barely hear it.

"Pop never could get that straight," he said. "My black belt's in karate, not judo."

"Well that's better," I said. "Even so, don't try anything fancy on your own. We've got to work together to pull this thing off."

"One question," he said.

"What?"

"You sound like you're pretty sure about Valencia."

"I don't know why, but I have the feeling he'll come along," I said. "He'll take some convincing, especially the part about taking Rosa to the American consul and not to the police, but for some reason I think he'll come with us."

"The Mexican brass won't like him freelancing," Suarez said.

"I know, but with him along we can claim that we came to Valencia with the warrant," I said. "We want to cover all the bases we can."

We made a nice soft landing at the Los Cabos airport. Without Espada to grease our way, we had to pass though the long lines of immigration like the rest of the *hoi polloi*. And to think that I used to be a VIP. We captured our luggage, grabbed two rental cars and made the familiar drive into Cabo San Lucas. I was tempted to stop and say hello to Brewster on the way in. But as much as I missed him I decided that it was best to follow my shrink's advice and keep my eye on the target. This was no time to get soft and mushy about my dog.

We were staying at a different hotel this time. I'd made myself notorious at the Hotel Sol. If I checked in there Rosa might hear about it.

Our new hotel, the Mar de Baja, was in the middle of town, a couple of blocks off Marina Boulevard. Family owned and operated for more than thirty years, it was one of the first hotels in Cabo. The architecture reflected the old colonial style that most of the modern hotels tried and usually failed to duplicate. It wasn't fancy, but it was good enough for what we needed. I liked the location, too. It was convenient to everything and had the double advantage of privacy. Parking was in a lot in back of the hotel and we didn't have to go through the lobby to get to our rooms. It didn't have the beach location or view of the Hotel Sol, but we weren't there for sightseeing.

We took adjoining rooms on the ground floor. Both rooms had patios leading to the pool. After I unpacked I called the hospital to check on Dottie. Doctor Padilla wasn't in, but I was told that while she still couldn't take calls, there was no change in her condition.

I walked next door and knocked on Suarez's door. He opened it, motioned me in and flopped on the bed, cradling his head against the ornately carved headboard.

"For the price, this is a nice place," he said. "I've got to remember it if I ever come back here."

"If you ever come back here you can stay with us," I said. "I'm going to contact Valencia and see if I can arrange a meeting tonight, then I'll call Eddie and set up something with him tomorrow morning. Why don't you go over to Pedregal, check in with your pals at the gate, and spread a little more of Taft's money around? See if anything's changed while we were gone. You might try to find out if Rosa has any kind of routine we might take advantage of, too."

"You got it." Suarez bounced to his feet in one smooth motion. "You want me around when you talk to Valencia?"

"I don't think so," I said. "It's better that I do it alone. He'll probably be skittish enough as it is without somebody he doesn't know there, too."

"In that case I'll catch dinner on my own." He raised his eyebrows. "I assume we're keeping a low profile, right?"

"Right," I said. "Stay out of the clubs for sure."

"After I talk to the guard, how about if I check out the climb to the house so we won't have any surprises when we do it?" he asked. "Nothing big, just a little reconnoiter."

"That's a good idea," I said. "You might see about recovering our guns, too. But don't go through the hotel lobby, and, like I said earlier, don't get too ambitious. It might be best to wait 'til after dark."

I gave him the directions to where I buried my Smith & Wesson.

"That should be easy enough," he said.

"Remember, don't let anybody see what you're doing," I said.

I was repeating myself. Suarez looked at me as if I'd turned into the village idiot.

"You really do think I'm an amateur, don't you?" he asked.

"Sorry," I apologized. "I'm just keyed up."

I opened the door to leave Suarez's room. "I'll either see you later tonight or early tomorrow."

Back in my room I called Valencia.

"They told me you left," he said. "There was no one at your home either, except a very large dog."

"I did leave, but only temporarily," I said. "How's my dog?"

"Healthy," he replied. "I have some questions about what happened to Miss Winthrop. I'm sure you know at least as much about it as I do, probably more. Where are you?"

"I just checked into the Mar de Baja," I said. "I want to talk to you, too., but unofficially How about dinner? Not one of the popular places. Someplace quiet and out of the way where tourists don't go. I know a few possibilities, but maybe you know someplace better."

"You don't want to be seen, is that correct?" he asked.

I didn't say anything. Apparently my silence was a sufficient answer.

"I know of such a place," he said. "I'll pick you up at your hotel."

"Okay," I said. "Meet me in the parking lot in back."

"At seven?"

"That's fine," I said.

Next call … Eddie Heenan.

I tried the Hotel Sol first. There was no answer in his room. Instead of leaving a message I tried his cell phone.

"Heenan."

"Eddie, it's Ethan Cruickshank."

"So where the hell are you now, Tierra del Fuego?"

"Is anybody close enough to hear your end of the conversation?"

"Hang on."

I heard some rustling noises, Eddie said something I couldn't make out, and there was what I thought might be the sound of a chair scraping on a hard surface.

A few seconds later, he said, "We're okay now. I walked out to the beach."

"Where were you?"

"At the bar at the hotel," he said. "I went fishing. When I got back I took a swim, changed clothes and came down to the bar to have a drink before dinner."

"How was the fishing?"

"Not good yesterday; great today. We hit everything!"

"I want to get together in the morning. Is breakfast okay?"

"Sure," he said. "What time?"

"How about eight?"

"Is anything in this town open that early?"

"Yeah, the restaurant where I'm staying opens at seven."

"Where's that?"

I told him. "You can either take a cab or drive. It's just a couple of minutes down the hill. A cab will save you having to look for it."

"If the restaurant doesn't mind shorts and running shoes I'll probably just run down and run back," he said.

"This is Cabo," I said. "You could show up in a kilt and an Indian headdress and they wouldn't say anything. But I've gotta warn you, Eddie, that hill's easy on the way down but it's absolute murder on the way back," especially on a full stomach."

"I've already done it a couple of times," he said. "It's a good workout."

"Any way you want it, Hercules," I said. "See you in the morning."

"You got it."

I thought of running up that hill - not unless I was being chased by some very bad people, and even then I might have second thoughts.

CHAPTER 40

VALENCIA'S white SUV wheeled into the crushed rock parking lot. I opened the door and climbed in. He was dressed in civilian clothes – a gray and white shirt, sandals and dark trousers. He didn't bother to shake hands.

"Where are we headed?" I asked.

"I have a cousin who owns a restaurant," he said. "I have arranged for a private room."

We headed out of town on the highway toward San Jose del Cabo. After about fifteen minutes, we turned left into the parking lot of a small restaurant that was set back from the highway. We drove around back and parked. It was an open-air restaurant with a palapa roof. There was a small two-story stucco building in back of the restaurant. My guess was that the owner probably lived there.

Valencia knocked on the back door. A chubby middle-aged man wearing a white apron covered with food stains opened the door and led us up a flight of stairs into a small room. The walls were painted white and floor was done in Saltillo tile. A big window offered a view of the restaurant roof below and the parking lot out front.

The highway beyond that was illuminated by the head-lights of the passing vehicles. The room had double-pane windows and good insulation so I couldn't hear anything from the restaurant below, which meant that nobody down there could hear us either.

Valencia and the man in the apron spoke to each other in Spanish and then the man in the apron went away.

"Sit down." Valencia motioned to a small table and two chairs by the window. There were no other furnish-ings in the room. "Jose will bring us menus."

Two minutes later, he did. After more Spanish, this time all of it spoken by Jose, Valencia asked, "Would you like something to drink?"

I ordered a margarita on the rocks. Valencia passed it on and Jose left. He reappeared a few minutes later with our drinks. Valencia was having iced tea.

"You're not drinking," I asked.

"Not tonight," he said.

I took a sip of my margarita. The combination of the tequila and the mild burn of the salt felt cleansing. I ran my tongue over my lips, took another sip, and put the margarita on the table.

"I am certain that the day you checked out was the happiest day in the long history of the Hotel Sol." Valencia started to smile and apparently thought better of it. "It seems that you were frightening the customers."

"I can only imagine," I said. "It's not the first time I've been bad for business."

Valencia nodded, his probing eyes never leaving my face.

"You have some questions for me," I said. "Fire away, I'm an open book."

"I doubt that very much," he said.

This time he did smile, even if it was only a mocking half smile. Good, I thought. I was making progress.

"Why don't you tell me your story, all of it this time?" he asked. "I've given you a great deal of latitude, but there will be no more, not after what happened to Miss Winthrop. You will tell me everything."

With a motion of his hand, Valencia indicated that I should get started.

I told him what brought me to live in Cabo San Lucas in the first place, the circumstances that led to my looking for Rosa, and about Dina being in France with her father.

I told him about the surfer dude who tracked me in the lobby of the Hotel Sol and how I followed him to his place. I didn't mention the guy in my room. He already knew about that.

I told him about the night meeting in the plaza, how I didn't show up and how I followed the girl and the twins to the Fiesta Mexicana.

I told him about recruiting Tony Suarez and gave him Suarez's background.

I told him about watching the girl for several days before I broke into her condo. I told him what I found there, including the multiple passports, the gun, the drugs, the mysterious reference to "A" at two thirty, and my narrow escape when she came back unexpectedly.

Valencia sighed and put his head in his hands. I didn't blame him. I was lucky. Stupid but lucky.

I told him about my accidental meeting with Dottie Winthrop in *Manana* and what she said about her contact with Rosa.

I told him about following the girl to the airport, seeing her meet Rosa and the brontosaurus, and Suarez following them into Pedregal.

I told him about our dinner with Dottie and how she filled us in on Rosa's house.

I told him about getting the late-night call from Doctor Padilla and driving to the hospital. I told him everything the doctor said, and my brief conversation with Dottie when she told me about the big dark man and what he did to her.

I told him about my meeting with Rosa on the jet skis and the deal we made.

I told him about Eddie Heenan coming down to Cabo and about the trouble he had in Mexico years ago. When I told him what Chango found out about Hector Macias, Valencia's eyes narrowed and his handsome face turned to flint.

I told him about my meeting with Taft.

"There," I said, "now you know everything."

"Not quite, I think," he said. "What are you planning to do now?"

We heard Jose trudging up the stairs. He approached our table. It was time to order. I hadn't taken a look at the menu yet. After a quick scan I ordered *El Ceviche Pobre*, fresh fish and small scallops prepared in lime, garlic, green chile, tomato and oregano, and grilled tuna medallions. Valencia ordered a mixed seafood salad with an herbal anchovy-pineapple vinaigrette and a flash fried whole red snapper.

I remarked that it seemed like an awfully upscale menu for a pretty basic sort of restaurant.

"It is," Valencia said. "Jose likes to keep his overhead low. The place is well known to the locals, those who can afford it, tourists who have discovered it, and now it is known to you. You are, after all, a local now, aren't you?"

I couldn't think of an easy way to get into what I wanted, so I just threw it on the table.

"I want to go into the Pedregal house and grab Rosa," I said. "And I want you to come with us."

This time Valencia laughed outright. He probably thought I was the funniest thing since the Three Stooges.

"And why would I do such a thing and break my own law?"

"Because we can get Rosa and Macias," I said. "If we wait for events to take their natural legal course between our countries, it won't happen. I think we both know that."

I explained the broad strokes of what I had in mind. When I told him about Heenan waiting at the Hotel Sol, Valencia smiled again.

"Unlike you, at least he hasn't shot anyone yet," he said.

He frowned when I explained my theory about his presence giving us legal cover. He obviously wasn't sure about that. I didn't blame him. I wasn't sure about it either. I worked like a son of a gun to be persuasive, but I couldn't tell if I was making any progress. I felt like a desperate salesman making a lousy cold call.

Our appetizers arrived. The ceviche was delicious. Valencia's salad looked good, too. He asked if I wanted another margarita. I said no.

Before Valencia started on his salad, he leaned forward so that his forearms were on the edge of the table, his fork in his right hand.

"You know, I could always have this Macias animal arrested," he said. "Wouldn't that be simpler and easier?"

"Yes, you could and it might," I agreed. "But he'd have a half-dozen people swear that on the night Dottie was beaten he was at home knitting a shawl for his poor feeble mother. I know he did it and you know he did it, but her ID isn't strong enough to hold up. A big guy with dark hair and eyebrows pretty much eliminates Woody Allen, but it still fits a helluva lot of other men."

Stabbing idly at his salad, Valencia thought it over.

"What about the ejaculation?" he asked. "If Doctor

Padilla kept a sample and the DNA matches Macias, then we would have him."

I hadn't thought of that. I'd been too focused on what I wanted. Valencia was right. The case would be virtually impossible to refute. The question was whether the case could be made at all.

"Even if the hospital took and kept a sample it might be too degraded," I said. "Remember that Dottie had to crawl a long way to get to the highway. Even if it worked, we might have Macias but we still wouldn't have Rosa. Forget about the drug thing and his association with *La Puerca*. I know that's not your problem. Your problem is that he'd get away to terrorize more women. I'm surprised he hasn't already. This doesn't have anything to do with sex. This guy's a predator."

I scored with that one. I could see it in Valencia's eyes. If I read him right, all he needed with the right push.

"Look, for all we know he's already back at his old habits," I said. "Maybe there are women out there who don't remember, or they know something happened but aren't sure what? That's the way it was before. Or maybe they do know and they're too ashamed to report it? That happens all the time., Rosa was at it for years before he finally got caught. Now he's in your town and this is our chance to bring him down."

Valencia rocked back and forth in his chair. The motion was almost imperceptible. I had him roiled up. He probably didn't even know he was doing it.

"It could end badly just as easily as it could end well," he said. "I can see the three of you in jail, a certain police lieutenant fired and in disgrace, and Rosa still free to do what he likes anywhere he wants to do it."

"I won't lie to you, there is that possibility," I admitted. "But remember, with Taft and his people we have a lot of clout on our side. Once the word got out there would be so much publicity in both countries that it would be very difficult for your government *not* to turn him over. And maybe the mysterious General Urrea will help. He seems to think you're hot stuff. In the meantime, yeah, it could turn sour on us, but I don't think so."

I reached across the table and grabbed Valencia's wrist. As tense as he was, I could feel the strength in his arm.

"Nothing is certain, but I believe that this will only work if you're with us," I said. "Without you, we'll just be three foreigners who've broken into the house of a wealthy and influential man who's broken no law here."

Valencia's eyes were hard and concentrated. The rocking had stopped and the room was still. The lights of the passing cars flickered on the highway. Jose had brought our food and it was sitting in front of us, but neither one of us had touched it.

"It may be madness. In fact, I'm sure that it is, but … yes, I will do it."

I didn't realize it, but I'd been holding my breath. I let in out in a long sigh.

"In that case," I said with a long sigh, "I think I'll have another margarita."

CHAPTER 41

We agreed to meet tomorrow morning at nine in my room at the Mar de Baja. I wanted to explain everything to Heenan at breakfast and then have him meet Suarez and Valencia.

I paid for dinner, left a fat tip for Jose, and Valencia drove me back to the hotel. It was late enough that there wasn't much traffic, although Cabo itself was at full bustle. As I expected, the Mar de Baja was quieter than the Hotel Sol. There was nobody in the lobby, in the halls, or even around the bar.

I knocked on Suarez's door.

"Who is it?"

"Bruce Springsteen," I said.

Humming "Born in the USA," Suarez opened the door. He was dressed in shorts and no shirt. His abdominal muscles looked like they were carved in granite. His knees were skinned and bloody.

"What the hell happened to you?" I asked.

I took a chair. He sat on the bed and reached for a small tube of salve on the bedside table.

"My reconnoiter was tougher than I thought," he explained. "Dottie was a little off about the location. Not much, but enough to make a difference. The house is over the cliff side of Pedregal, not the beach side. It's not far, but enough to make a difference. I had to go part way up the path and then climb sideways and go up some more to get there. It's doable, but it wasn't one of my more brilliant ideas to try it in the dark the first time. On the way back some dirt and rocks came out from under me and I thought I was going to slide all the way down to the damn beach. I ripped out both knees of my pants. Trust me, it'll be a lot easier in the daytime."

Suarez squirted the clear salve on one knee and spread it around with his index finger. He picked up a big square bandage that was ready on the bedside table, centered it on his knee, and patted it flat.

"It *is* doable though?" I asked.

"Oh, yeah. No question about it."

"Will anybody be able to see us going up from the beach?"

"It's hard to tell at night but I don't think so, not so it matters," he said, smearing salve on the other knee. "There's a lot of scrub and rock. In fact, it's all scrub and rock. If you were on the beach or out on a boat, had binoculars and knew we were up there you probably could see something, but why would anybody be doing that? And even if they did, so what?"

"And you're positive nobody saw you despite all the noise you must have made when you fell?"

Suarez snorted as he squared the bandage on his knee. "Like I said, it was dark. The noise wasn't that bad anyway. By the way, you're right about hiding under the pool deck. That's our spot. I got up there and checked it out."

"Jesus, Tony, I told you not ...."

Suarez raised his hand to stop me. "It's all right, fearless leader. Nobody saw me. They were otherwise engaged."

"What does 'otherwise engaged' mean?"

"Your girlfriend was in the pool with Rosa." Suarez grinned at the memory. "They were having a dandy little time. Pretty noisy about it, too. I took a chance and poked my head up over the side of the deck to see if they were doing what I thought they were doing. You might say I caught them at a critical moment. I could have landed a helicopter on the pool deck and they wouldn't have noticed."

I leaned back in the chair and looked at the ceiling. Calm down, Cruickshank, calm down. Yes, the kid took a ridiculous risk, but it was no more idiotic than my breaking into the girl's condo. There was no damage done, so I let it pass.

"She's a screamer, by the way," he laughed. "Makes a helluva racket."

I didn't say anything, mostly because there was nothing to say.

"I got our guns," He motioned toward the dresser. "Yours is in the top drawer."

I opened the drawer and took out my Smith & Wesson. It was still wrapped in the Hotel Sol towels. I unwrapped the towels and checked it out. Good as ever. The boxes of shells were there, too.

"Since you have such a keen ear and eye for detail, could you tell if anybody else was there?" I asked.

"I think the brontosaurus was inside," he replied. "I saw a big shadow pass across one of the windows. I didn't see his face or anything, but there aren't many people that size."

"He's probably stays close to Rosa all the time," I said. "See anybody else?"

"No, but that doesn't mean they weren't there. It's a pretty big house."

"Did you talk to the guards?"

Suarez got up, walked around the room and did a couple of deep knee bends to make sure that his handiwork stuck to his knees before returning to his place on the bed.

"Of course. I gave 'em another three hundred to spread around. By now they think we're the coolest thing going, better than an ATM. There's some bad news, though. According to the guards, all of Rosa's gang is staying in the Pedregal house now. That makes Rosa, the girl, the brontosaurus, the surfer dude and the twins."

That *was* bad news. I'd hoped that our leaving Cabo would relax Rosa and make him overconfident. Instead he'd pulled everybody in around him.

I told Suarez what I thought.

He nodded. "Yeah, I think he's scared, even if he thinks he bribed you out of town. Maybe he can't believe you found him and then handled the guy in your room. It probably scared the hell out of him. Having the brontosaurus do what he did to Dottie is the sign of a frightened man."

"Think he might be scared enough to clear out?" I asked.

"There's no way to tell," Suarez said. "He seems to have a considerable investment in real estate here, like he wanted to put down some roots. But he's rich enough to take a loss and laugh at it. To be safe, we should make our move pretty soon."

I didn't like the news about everybody moving into the Pedregal house, but there wasn't anything I could do about it.

"All things considered, I'd say you had a busy night," I said.

"I sure did," he said. "How'd you do with Valencia?"

"He's in," I said. "We'll all get together in my room tomorrow morning at nine, after I have breakfast with Heenan."

When he heard that Valencia was with us, Suarez yelled, "Yes!" and pounded the top of his knee with his fist. Bad move. He winced and bounced up and down on the bed.

"Damn, that hurt," he complained.

"I bet it did," I said.

I was not very sympathetic. It served the kid right.

CHAPTER 42

"SO WHEN ARE WE GOING IN?"

True to his word, Heenan had jogged from the Hotel Sol. He wore white shorts, a pair of light blue Nike jogging shoes, and a T-shirt that advertised the Hotel Sol fishing fleet. The lower part of his face that wasn't covered by sunglasses during his two days of fishing was burned a bright red. With the pale circles around his eyes, he looked like a raccoon in reverse.

I was so wrapped up in the conversation with Valencia that I hadn't eaten much last night and I was hungry. By the time Heenan arrived I was halfway through a ham and cheese omelet, potatoes, whole wheat toast, orange juice and coffee. Heenan shamed me with a disgusting healthy breakfast of dry cereal, yogurt, and orange juice.

"You're okay with it then?" I asked.

Heenan had mixed the cereal and yogurt in his bowl. To me, it looked about as appetizing as something you'd use to patch a hole in your wall. He spooned the last of it in his mouth and washed it down with orange juice. It was early by Cabo standards so we were the only customers in the restaurant.

"It could be better, but it could be worse, too," he said. "At least we don't have to guess when Rosa might be there. From what the kid learned it sounds like he's there all the time, at least for the time being. I like it that he's scared, too. I don't like it that he's got so many people with him, but there isn't anything we can do about it. The house sounds like it'll be hard to get to from the back, but that works in our favor. They won't expect anything from that way, if they expect anything at all. Given all that, what you've come up with sounds like the best we're gonna get, especially if we're gonna make our move soon."

"I guess what we have to ask ourselves is if the gain is worth the risk," I said.

Heenan raised his long arms above his head and stretched backward in his chair until his arms were parallel with the floor. I heard a lot of popping and cracking from his back. It sounded like firecrackers going off somewhere far away. After a couple of lunges backward while he stretched as far as he could, Heenan sighed with satisfaction and returned to a normal position.

"In my business, I ask myself that a lot," he said. "The thing is, if I decided it was too risky too often I'd have to find another line of work. I don't have many regrets in life, but those I have are mostly about things I *didn't* do. Waiting for the perfect time won't get us anywhere because the perfect time might never come. If we pull out now everything that's happened will be for nothing. You don't want that and neither do I."

I looked at my watch. It was nine.

"You ready to meet Suarez and Valencia?" I asked.

"Lead on," he said.

I signed the check. We left the restaurant and walked across the pool deck to my room on the other side.

Although it was early, the humidity was heavy in the air. It reminded me of the first time Dina and I came to Cabo. It was July and it was as humid as it was hot. I never sweat so much, or appreciated air conditioning so much, in my life.

I opened the screen and glass slider and walked into the room. Suarez and Valencia got to their feet and I introduced Heenan.

They didn't say anything, but I could see all three men size each other up as if they'd just had their testosterone tank topped off.

To Suarez, Heenan said, "You're Chango's kid. You're the, uh …."

"Queer?" There was an edge in Suarez's voice. Valencia noticed it, too. It was a challenge, vague and unspecific, but it was there.

"Actually I was gonna say the cop who'd rather be a lawyer," Heenan said. "I'm not sure that's a good trade. At least being a cop is honest work."

Suarez didn't try to cover his gaffe, or laugh it off.

"Are you suggesting that maybe I shouldn't jump to conclusions?" he asked.

"Maybe not," Heenan said. "Chango's told me about you."

"Your name's come up, too," Suarez said.

"Nothing good, I bet," Heenan said. "That's probably why you expected me to be a horse's ass."

"You've got that right," Suarez said. "You're not exactly on Pop's Christmas card list."

"Chango and I bump heads sometimes," Heenan said. "He wants one thing and I usually want something else. The old bastard's a good cop, though."

"He's the best," Suarez declared.

"Probably," Heenan agreed. "He's a man, too. He

won't say one thing and do another. You always know where you stand with Chango."

The challenge was gone now. Valencia took it all in with his usual mocking half-smile. Not for the first time, I thought that this was an odd team I'd put together, probably because I didn't really put it together. It seemed to assemble itself.

I decided that it was time to tell them what Taft told me. Valencia already knew. The others didn't.

"Gentleman, I have some information that two of you haven't heard." I repeated my conversation with Taft. "I don't blame you if this changes things. If anybody wants out now is the time."

I looked from face to face. Suarez shook his head, Valencia's half smile reappeared, and Heenan, as usual had something to say.

"Like I told you before, as long as the money's good I don't care who pays the bills."

We spent the next two hours going over everything we knew about the house, including the photos we got from Dottie, what we knew about the people we faced, and Suarez's observations from his climb last night. Everybody agreed that my plan to go in with Valencia in the front and the rest of us from the back probably was the best of our options.

"We want to try to hustle Rosa into Valencia's SUV and get him to the American consul's office." I turned to Valencia. "You know where that is, right?"

Valencia nodded. "My people won't like it, but I think you're right to do it that way."

"Hector will be the toughest nut to crack," I said. "Tony and I will take him. That leaves the rest for you two."

Heenan and Valencia looked at each other across the room.

"That's what, four to two," Heenan said. "Five if you count the girl." He stared at Valencia. "What do you think?"

"Perhaps you should take the girl while I handle the rest," Valencia said.

Heenan's eyes lit up. He looked any happier it would have been Christmas.

"You'll do," he said.

Heenan turned back to me.

"There is one thing," he said. "I don't think we ought to go in there with just our dicks in our hands. You never know what they might come up with. One of us ought to be carrying. Don't use it unless they do, but it might be good to have, just in case."

I looked at Valencia and Suarez to see what they thought. Without saying anything, they indicated that they agreed.

"Valencia then," I said. "As a cop, he can carry with no legal problems. But I don't want it visible. They might get rattled if they see it and start something we don't want right away. Remember, we want Rosa alive."

"Something else," Heenan asked. "When Valencia goes through the gate he'll have to identify himself. What's to stop the guards from calling Rosa to tell him he's on the way?"

"First, I'll order them to say nothing," Valencia said. "I'll tell them that if Rosa is warned I'll have their *cojones*."

"And second, more grease," added Suarez. "They've cooperated so far. Remember, they don't like Rosa anyway. I'll go back today, make another payment, and tell 'em there's more if they keep quiet."

Suarez tilted his head toward Valencia. "Between his threats and my cash, it ought to be okay, especially since they don't like Rosa anyway."

"All right, then," I said. "All that's left is when."

"ASAP," said Heenan.

I saw more agreement in the eyes of Valencia and Suarez.

Just like that, I decided.

"Tomorrow afternoon at two thirty," I said. "They're not going out so they're probably not sleeping late. Especially if this humidity holds, maybe we'll catch them at siesta time or hanging around the pool."

"Or both," Suarez said. "Unless they carry guns in their bathing suits, around the pool would be a good thing."

"What about last night?" I asked. "Could you tell if they were carrying?"

"All I can tell you is that the happy duo in the pool weren't wearing bathing suits," he said.

"Good point," I said.

CHAPTER 43

THE TIME PASSED SO SLOWLY it was if it didn't pass at all. The more I tried not to think about what we were about to do, the more I thought about it. I slept eight hours that night, but that still left a lot of time to kill.

I killed most of it by hanging around the pool and reading. Now I was working on "Desolation Island," one of Patrick O'Brian's naval novels about Captain Jack Aubrey and his friend, surgeon Stephen Maturin. Eventually I got so bored that I went into the Mar de Baja's small workout room and slaved away at the Nautilus torture rack. As something to do, it was marginally better than clipping my fingernails.

Suarez spent most of the time sleeping, swimming, and watching TV, including a bunch of DVDs he cadged from the hotel desk. Unfortunately they were in Spanish, which did me no good in terms of entertainment value.

I had no idea what Heenan and Valencia did, although Valencia was probably on duty part of the time.

I called Dina, but I hoped that no one would answer. I didn't want to tell her that D Day had arrived, but I didn't want to lie to her either. I got my wish. No one answered. Her father didn't have an answering machine so I didn't even have to leave a message.

I called Dottie at the hospital, too. After the usual shuffle, this time I actually got her.

"Well hello, Mister Private Eye. Who are you today?

Her voice was much stronger. So was her sense of humor.

"Today I'm Ellery Queen."

"That's too bad. I never linked Ellery Queen. Too prissy."

"Miles Archer?"

"Who the hell is Miles Archer?"

"He was Sam Spade's partner in 'The Maltese Falcon.'"

"The one who got shot?"

"Yeah."

"That's probably not your best choice."

"I take it from the banter that you're feeling better."

"Lots," she said. "The doctor says I can probably go home in a few days."

"Oh, yeah. When?"

"That he wouldn't say. Just 'in a few days.' You know how doctors are. How are *you* doing?"

"Good," I said. "We're making progress."

"What does that mean?"

"Don't say anything, but it looks like things will come to a head in the next day or two. I don't want to say any more right now."

"Interesting," she said. "You watch yourself, Miles Archer."

"You, too," I said.

"Don't worry," she said. "I've got a whole hospital that does it for me."

CHAPTER 44

WE MET at the Mar de Baja at one thirty. I called Taft to tell him we were going in and he reminded me to make my two calls when we finished, no matter how it ended.

Valencia drove us to the Hotel Sol in his SUV. Except for the humidity, it was a beautiful day. The few clouds looked like cotton candy. The sky was such a startling blue that it seemed like a new and different color. When three of us got out of the SUV at the Hotel Sol, even though I couldn't see the ocean I felt it looming on the other side of the hotel.

I walked around to the driver's side of the SUV. The window whirred down. I leaned over and put my forearms on the roof. It was hot to the touch, but I'm so damn manly that I ignored it.

"Remember, ring the door bell at exactly two thirty," I said. "We'll give you three minutes before we move in."

Valencia flashed his mocking half smile. "I have no doubt that it will be the longest three minutes of my life."

He was diplomatic enough not to mention that we'd already gone over everything at least five times. I was jumpy. We all were.

I stepped back from the SUV. The window went up and Valencia pulled away.

I turned to Heenan and Suarez.

"Okay, it's show time," I said.

We skirted the hotel lobby and walked down to the beach. There was no one there. For one thing it was siesta time. In Cabo, even tourists fell into the siesta habit. For another it was too hot and humid. If you had to be outside, a pool was the place to be. The surf was running high and the waves pounded the shore with such force that we could feel the vibration in our feet.

My shirt was soaked before I took fifty steps. I wiped my forehead with the back of my hand. Heenan was sweating as much as I was. His pullover shirt was practically soaked through, too. Suarez looked a little warm, but that was all. Where Heenan and I left deep footprints as we plowed along the beach, Suarez seemed to glide over the top of the sand with the slightly pigeon-toed walk that a lot of top athletes have.

After about three-quarters of a mile, Suarez turned up toward the hills leading to Pedregal.

"We'll go about halfway up, maybe a little less, then move off to the right," he explained. "It gets a lot tougher then."

Suarez led the way, with me following and Heenan bringing up the rear. This part was was easy. After all, it was designed so that the people who lived in Pedregal could walk down to the beach. Looking up, I could see three or four of the big houses looming at the top. To the right, our gentle hill turned into a nasty looking climb. It wasn't really a cliff, but it was so steep that we'd be on all fours a lot of the way, using our hands to pull ourselves up the mix of rock, dirt, sand and scrubby brush.

"I can't believe you climbed that in the dark," I told Suarez.

"Now that I see it in the daylight I'm pretty impressed myself," he admitted.

From the rear, Heenan rumbled, "Kid, you must be a lot dumber than you look."

About halfway up the hill Suarez left the path and moved to the right so that we were going up and sideways at the same time. Sometimes it was more sideways than up. There was no trail anymore so we had to make our own, grabbing whatever we could to pull ourselves higher. What looked like solid rock had a disconcerting way of crumbling when I put my weight on it. Several times I slid down four or five feet before I was able to catch myself. A couple of times I almost knocked Heenan off his feet.

Of the three of us, Suarez had the easiest time. He was smaller and lighter than we were and seemed to effortlessly move from one spot to the next. It was harder for me, but I kept up okay. Heenan was struggling and quickly fell behind. For once his size worked against him. His weight caused the rocks to break apart and start a series of small slides. Several times he grabbed a ragged looking bush or a handful of scraggly weeds and it came out by the roots, which left him cursing and sliding until he caught himself on something else.

"I feel like a fucking mountain goat," he grumbled.

"A mountain goat would have an easier time of it," I said. "It'd be a lot quieter, too. I hope we're not making as much noise as it sounds like we are."

Three-quarters of the way up, Suarez motioned us to stop. Moving quietly, with precise placement of his hands and feet, he came back to us.

"From now on no talking," he whispered. "Pretty soon you'll be able to see the pool deck where it sticks out over the edge. Ethan, put your hands and feet where I do. Eddie, you put your hands and feet where Ethan does.

Test whatever you put your feet on to make sure it'll support you before you put your full weight on it. It'll be slower, but we've got plenty of time. When we get to the top we're gonna hide under the deck like we planned."

Suarez took the lead again. We were careful to test each hand and foothold. By now, my hands were raw and bleeding. Heenan's were probably just as bad.

I was concentrating so hard on the climb and not making noise that we were there before I knew it.

According to the photographs the pool was more or less oval, with big concrete columns supporting the deck around the pool. The bottom of the deck was at least twelve feet above where we were standing. The pool and deck made a peninsula that was connected to the rest of patio on the side closest to the house, opposite of where we were.

I was breathing so heavily that it took a while to bring it under control. Other than the perspiration that soaked his shirt and dripped off his chin, Suarez might have been taking a walk in the park. His breathing was even and regular. Heenan looked like he'd gone two out of three falls with Fred the Fighting Anaconda.

I looked at my watch. We had ten minutes until Valencia was supposed to ring the door bell. On the right side of the pool, steps made of old railroad ties went up to the deck. Probably nobody but a maintenance man ever came down here. Looking around, I wasn't sure why even a maintenance man would bother. There didn't seem to be anything to maintain. The pool equipment must be on the other side where we couldn't see it.

We each picked a column to lean against, careful to keep out of sight in case someone leaned over the white wrought iron railing that bordered the deck and looked down, although that didn't seem very likely. To see us, they've have to bend so far over they'd risk falling over. They'd probably roll all the way down to the beach.

This high there was a nice breeze off the ocean. I pulled my sweat-sticky shirt away from my chest to try and cool off. I could see several boats out on the bright blue water, fishing boats probably. They were too far away to tell for sure.

I checked my watch again. Only three minutes had passed. I saw Suarez and Heenan doing the same thing. I tried to imagine what we'd find up there. There was no telling, but trying to imagine the possibilities and combinations at least gave me something to do. I could hear music coming from the pool, mostly a thumping base line. Rap. I'd discovered yet another reason to dislike Andy Rosa; he had lousy taste in music.

Moving quietly and carefully, Suarez crawled to the stairs on all fours. Heenan looked a question at me, but I just shrugged. I had no idea what Suarez was up to. Sitting on the bottom step, he reached behind the pillar that was closest to the steps and came out with one of those viewing gizmos that people use when there's a big crowd at a golf tournament and they want to see over the heads. It was about three feet long. The top was bent one way and the bottom another. There was a series of mirrors inside so that you could look in one end and see out the other. Suarez must have bought it at one of the Cabo golf courses, brought it with him when he made his night climb and left it to use later. Smart kid.

He got to his feet, moved up three or four steps and slowly eased the gizmo above his head until the top was just over the lip of the deck. It was like using a periscope. Ever so slowly, he turned one way, then the other. Satisfied, he lowered the gizmo, put it back in its hiding place, and carefully made his way to us.

"Five around the pool; Rosa, Hector, the surfer dude,

and the twins," he whispered. "I didn't see the girl. Maybe she's inside. Rosa and Hector are on the other side of the pool. The others are on this side with their backs to us."

So the whole team was there, with the possible exception of the girl. Too bad. I looked at my watch again. Two minutes to go. Of course, I'd told Valencia that we wouldn't move until three minutes after he rang the bell, so we had five minutes before we made our move. I was certain we'd hear the door bell, even down here. In a place like Cabo where everybody spends so much time outdoors, it would do no good to have a door bell that could be heard only indoors.

I motioned for all three of us to go up the stairs. I wanted to be in the best possible position to hear the bell. When we settled on the three top steps, I looked at my watch. Less than a minute to go. I felt like I was ready to explode. Suarez and Heenan looked the way I felt. I could feel a tingling along my scalp. Goose bumps, too.

The bell was louder than I expected, the standard three note chimes. A woman's voice came from just inside the house. She said something in Spanish. Suarez whispered a translation: "She told Hector to go to the door, but to let her answer it. It's kind of strange that she's giving orders."

Heenan looked at his watch again, waiting for the minutes to tick off. I heard the slapping sound of flip-flops across the deck and into the house.

After a short silence, I heard the girl's voice again.

"She told Rosa there's a cop who wants to talk to him about a burglary at the house next door," Suarez said. "She's bringing him back here. That's pretty smart of Valencia."

"Twenty seconds," mouthed Heenan silently.

I heard footsteps on the deck followed by another scraping sound. Rosa said something in Spanish.

"He asked Valencia if he'd like something to drink," Suarez whispered.

Heenan cut in. "Now!"

We went up the steps in single file. This time I led, followed by Suarez and Heenan. At the top on the left was a gate in the same white wrought iron pattern. Like the fence, the gate was about four feet high. I put my hand on the top and vaulted over.

With their attention on Valencia, they didn't see us coming until we were well inside the fence. The girl saw us first. She was barefoot, wearing a white bikini, and standing beside Valencia, who was on the other side of the pool facing Rosa, who had his back to us. She froze for an instant as her eyes met mine. Sometime about her manner alerted Rosa. He turned around and saw us, too. They both screamed, "Hector!" at the same time.

CHAPTER 45

THE SURFER DUDE and the twins were on our left. With the surfer dude leading, they rose out of their chaise lounges and started toward us. Heenan peeled off to intercept them.

Across the pool, Valencia grabbed Rosa's arm above the elbow. The girl stepped back to give herself room, assumed a karate stance for balance, extended her long leg, and with a loud slap caught Valencia on the side of his face with her bare foot. Although he staggered from the blow and let go of Rosa, Valencia looked more surprised than hurt. When she made the same move, only from the opposite direction with the other leg, Valencia was ready. He caught her ankle with both hands, gave an up and sideways heave that put her flat on her back with a nasty "splat" that knocked the wind out of her.

Hector came charging out of the house and immediately got all of my attention. It was like watching the charge of a bull elephant, except bull elephants don't wear knee-length plaid shorts and a T-shirt with the arms cut off. Hector headed toward Rosa and the girl but Suarez and I cut him off. With Suarez on his right and me on his left, Hector went into a defensive crouch with his arms spread wide and his head moving back and forth from Suarez to me and back again. When Hector turned toward me Suarez exploded from down low. Driving forward with all the strength in his legs, he clipped Hector behind the knee with his shoulder. Hector sagged, but he didn't go down. Moving fast for such a big man, he whirled around and kicked Suarez hard in the shoulder. Suarez rolled away and scrambled to his feet, flexing his shoulder. First round to the big man.

While Hector was distracted I got in close and hit him three times on the eye and the side of the face with the heel of my hand. He jerked around, extended his left arm like a two-by-four and caught me across the chest with a blow that sent me sprawling.

He was on me before I could get to my feet. He grabbed a handful of my shirt and yanked me up, clubbing me in the side of the head with his other hand. He folded one arm around me, brought me close, and brought his other arm around for a bear hug that would probably break my back. His breath stank like a festering sump. Before he could get the bear hug closed Suarez got hold of his wrist. It took all of Suarez's strength to keep that huge arm from closing. With my free arm, I smashed Hector in the middle of the face with my elbow and blood erupted from his broken nose. Enraged by the pain, he let out a deep primeval roar and flung Suarez away. When he did that I slipped out of his grasp, dropped to the deck, rolled away and got back on my feet. Hector shuffled back a couple of steps to give himself room. Suarez's right eye was swollen. I could taste blood in my mouth.

As we circled Hector I caught glimpses of the rest of the fight. With the surfer dude hanging onto his back and clawing at his face, Heenan pressed one of the twins over his head and threw him over the fence and down the cliff we'd just climbed. On the other side of the pool, Valencia had his forearm locked around Rosa's throat. Using the struggling Rosa for balance, Valencia left his feet and kicked the other twin in the chest, which sent him skidding across the deck on his butt. The girl was struggling to get up but having a hard time of it. I could hear her wheezing as she fought to get her wind back.

Seeing Rosa in trouble, Hector's massive chest expanded as he took a deep breath.

"Tony," I yelled as Hector charged Suarez to get to Rosa. Suarez rolled sideways into Hector's knees at the same time I barreled into his massive back with my shoulder and forearm. It was like running into the side of a building but the combination of our weights going in different directions finally took him off his feet. He fell forward over Suarez and I rolled over his head and bounced to my feet. Suarez was up, too, although one arm was hanging awkwardly at his side. As Hector started to get up Suarez gave him an expert stiff-legged kick in the throat. Hector made a croaking sound and fell backward, only to rise again with his arms spread wide like an angry grizzly bear.

We came at him again, Suarez from his right and me from his left. All of my concentration was on the three of us, as if there was no one else in the world. By now we were covered in sweat, blood and grime. Suarez's kick to Hector's throat must have hurt him. His mouth was open and his breath was hard and rasping.

Suarez put a side kick into Hector's gut. For all the effect it had he might as well have sent him flowers. I got in a kick to his groin. It hit the target and I felt him shudder, but he ignored whatever pain he felt and grabbed me by the throat with one hand and started clubbing me with the other, hard body shots that felt like I was getting hit with a lead pipe. With one of the blows, I felt something snap on my left side. I was so pumped up that it didn't hurt, but knew that I had a broken rib. I got in three good punches, two to his throat and one to his face, but Hector's strength seemed endless.

Suarez forced Hector to break his hold on my throat by gouging his eyes. With another roar, Hector dropped me and Suarez pumped four more hard shots into his solar plexus. Hector clubbed Suarez on the back of his head and he went down on his hands and knees. From where Hector had dropped me I drove forward and up. Using all the strength in my legs I put my shoulder in his gut and he went over backward.

As he fell Suarez was on top of him with crisp hard rights that made Hector groan. I was pounding away, too. I wasn't even sure what I was hitting anymore. Every molecule in my body was concentrated on the punches.

Hector threw us off and we got to our feet. Suarez shirt was torn off and his face and chest was running with blood. My ribs were hurting, and I knew that I was a mess, too.

Hector tried to get up, but his movements were slow and ponderous, like he wasn't in complete control of his limbs. He managed to get to one knee, balancing himself with one hand on the deck, when Suarez planted his left foot, pivoted, raised his leg and in a motion that was too fast to follow put the heel of his foot in Hector's face. Hector wavered for a moment, then toppled over and fell on his back. It was like watching a buffalo fall after it had been shot.

Through swollen lips, Suarez stood over the fallen Hector and said, "Dottie Winthrop says hello, you fat tub of guts."

I felt dull and slow. There was a ringing in my head and my ribs hurt. It took a moment before I remembered what I was supposed to do. I reached for my cell phone in its holster on my belt, but it wasn't there. As I looked around the deck trying to find it a dozen police stormed out of the house. Their weapons were drawn and they were barking orders I didn't understand.

They had me wrapped up before I could find my phone. It was over. We had failed.

CHAPTER 46

I HAD TWO BROKEN RIBS. Suarez had a dislocated shoulder. He also had some stitches, plus a variety of aches and pains. So did I, only not as many stitches. We exchanged this information from adjoining hospital beds in St. Luke's.

I remembered being taken to the hospital. When a nurse asked me where I was hurt, I replied, "All over." After that, I slept. They probably gave me a shot to put me out. There were no clocks in the room, but when I woke up I knew that I had been out for a while. That was when I discovered Suarez was in the bed next to me. He didn't know any more than I did, although he did remember hearing one of the nurses say that we must have been in an automobile accident.

The left side of Suarez's face was swollen and his eye was a slit. The swelling and stitches inside his mouth muffled his speech, too.

I mentioned that he looked extraordinarily ugly.

"Just be glad you can't see yourself," he mumbled. "It ain't pretty."

There was a cop outside the door to our room. I told Suarez to ask the cop if I could make a telephone call.

When Suarez made the request, the cop laughed. I took that to mean no.

Little by little, we began piecing it together. The more information we got the worse it looked. Suarez and I were in the hospital, Heenan was in jail, and Valencia was suspended without pay. If it weren't for our injuries, Suarez and I would be in jail with Heenan.

On the plus side, a nurse who spoke English told me that Hector was in the hospital, too, along with the twin that Heenan threw down the cliff, and their injuries were much worse than ours. She scolded both of us with a frown when she saw our satisfied smiles. I asked her about the other twin, the surfer dude, the girl, and Rosa, but she only shrugged. Either she didn't know any more or my charm was losing its power. Suarez suggested that both were distinct possibilities.

Heenan, Suarez and I were charged with illegal entry, kidnapping and illegal detainment. I had no idea why Valencia wasn't charged, too, but I assumed they'd get around to him.

"I don't get these charges," Suarez complained. He sounded like his mouth was full of cotton. "How can we be charged with illegal detainment *and* kidnapping? Besides, we never took him anywhere. How can you kidnap someone when you never have them in your possession?"

"Well, the illegal entry charge is sorta true," I admitted. "For the other stuff, maybe they count Valencia's arm around Rosa's throat as illegal detainment?"

There *was* some good news. We found out that Rosa, the twin who wasn't in the hospital, and the surfer dude were all in custody, too, while the authorities tried to sort it all out. Nobody seemed to know anything about the girl.

Unfortunately an incident in jail did not help our

cause. This bit of unwelcome information came from Doctor Padilla, as did a lot of what we found out. It turned out that Heenan was thrown into a cell with four other men. The accommodations consisted of a twelve by twelve concrete room with an overflowing toilet in one corner that probably hadn't worked since the days of Pancho Villa. Three of the walls were concrete. The fourth wall was made of iron bars that opened to a hallway lined with a half-dozen other cells.

Rosa was being escorted past Heenan's cell to talk to his lawyer. Heenan was standing at the bars, a space that he had carved out as his own because it was as far away from the toilet as possible. According to Padilla, Heenan's negotiation with the other prisoners for the space was "of a physical nature."

As he passed Heenan, Rosa sneered, "I'll piss on your grave, shit head," and spit on him. Unfortunately for Rosa, Heenan's arm was longer, and his reactions quicker, than Rosa thought. Heenan reached through the bars and grabbed Rosa by his shirt. Moving that big arm rapidly back and forth like a piston, he beat Rosa against the bars three or four times before the police broke his hold. It took three of them to do it and even they they had to practically break his wrist. By then Rosa was semi-conscious. Now he was in St. Luke's, too, on a different floor. At the rate we were going, we might fill up the place. Heenan's wrist was treated and he was returned to jail, this time in solitary confinement.

Which explains how Heenan was also charged with assaulting a prisoner.

I was lying in my bed staring at the ceiling tiles and Suarez was watching a soccer broadcast out of Mexico City on an old black and white TV high on the wall when Taft and Espada walked into the room, along with a Mexican army officer in full glorious uniform and what I took to be two uniformed aides walking a couple of steps behind. There was no smoking in the hospital, but Espada had an unlit cigarette dangling from his lips.

The cop at the door said something that sounded like a protest. The officer looked at him like he was an insect, jerked his head and one of the aides dragged the cop out the door and down the hall. The other one reached up and turned off the television.

Taft walked to the side of my bed.

"You didn't make the call," he said.

"I couldn't," I said. "I lost the phone in the fight. We didn't get the job done."

"Rosa's in custody," he said.

"Yeah, but it's not what we wanted," I said. "The police are not happy with us. By the time his lawyers get through with it, he'll be Little Red Riding Hood we'll be a bunch of big bad wolves. The Mexican government's probably not thrilled either. It'll make getting Rosa back to the United States a lot harder."

"It *is* a hell of a mess," Taft agreed.

As we talked, my eyes kept turning to the Mexican officer. I couldn't help it. Even standing still with his hands clasped behind his back, he seemed to radiate power. He was short, probably not more than five six or seven, but held himself so erect that he seemed much taller. He had gray hair and a weathered face and dominated the room without trying. There was something about Taft's body language that told me that even he deferred to this man.

"One thing I can't figure out is how the police got there so quickly," I said.

"The girl," Taft answered.

"What?"

"Espada was told that the house had an alarm that went off at the police station," he said. "Most of the houses up there have a similar set up. When she recovered from being knocked on her ass by your friend she ran inside the house and triggered the alarm. My guess is that she saw how it was going and figured that getting the police there was better than having you drag Rosa away."

That made sense. I didn't see her when I looked around for my cell phone.

"Where is she now?" I asked.

Taft shrugged. "Nobody knows. She disappeared. Wherever she went, she hasn't used any of the passports you saw, so she's probably still in Mexico."

"We've been told Valencia's suspended," I said. "Is that true?"

"Yes, it is," he said. "They're not happy with him. This thing should go to court in a few days. We're working on it."

"By the way, that ugly gentleman in the next bed is Tony Suarez," I said.

Taft didn't bother to turn around. For all he cared, the guy in the next bed could have been Cesar Romero.

Without warning, the officer stepped up to the side of my bed. Taft stepped back.

"Tell me about Valencia," he said.

I looked at Taft, who nodded that it was okay to answer.

"What do you want to know?"

"How did he do ... his behavior."

"Couldn't have been better," I said. "I put him in an awkward position but he handled it well. He was honorable all the way through. I would work with him again anytime. I don't know how he feels about what happened, or how bad his situation is. Whatever trouble he's in is my fault. He's a good cop and a good man."

The officer looked at me for a long time. I felt my face

grow warm. He finally nodded, turned on his heel and left the room.

"Who the hell was that?" I asked, although I already knew the answer.

"That was General Urrea," said Taft as he turned to follow Urrea out the door.

"Couple of real nice guys," Suarez said once they left. "It was a pleasure to meet them."

CHAPTER 47

EVENTS MAY HAVE BEEN INFLUENCED by all the newspaper and television reporters who swarmed Cabo San Lucas when they found out what happened.

I assumed that Taft had a lot to do with their finding out, or at least getting the word out faster than it might have otherwise. At first the story was regional, confined mostly to Southern California. Then it went national, which increased the pressure on the Mexican government. What went on behind the scenes I have no idea, although I'm sure something did.

What I do know is that the charges against us were dismissed.

Then, after three weeks of indecipherable legal gobbledygook, Andy Rosa was shipped back to the United States. The official explanation was that there is a provision in Mexican immigration law that denies entry into the country to a person with a foreign criminal warrant against them. In effect, Andy Rosa was an illegal alien. Enforcement of that provision is what you might call highly discretionary. But this time it came in handy because it gave the Mexican government a way out without looking like it was kowtowing to the United States.

As for the rest of the Rosa's merry little band, it turned out that the twins were wanted for a variety of charges in both the U. S. and Mexico and the two countries began another fight over who had jurisdiction. The surfer dude, who wasn't wanted by anybody, quickly broke down under the gentle questioning by Mexican police and confessed that Hector Macias was the one who attacked Dottie Winthrop, which took care of Hector for a long time.

In short, it was over.

CHAPTER 48

Dina and I were outside on our patio overlooking the spot where the Pacific meets the Sea of Cortez. Actually it's probably just the Pacific, but I like it better the other way because it sounds more romantic. It was late in the afternoon, the sunlight was dancing on the ocean and a light breeze had cut the heat. My ribs didn't hurt anymore and it was one of those moments that you'd like to put away somewhere so you could bring it out whenever you want it.

I was sitting in an Adirondack chair facing the ocean. Brewster was on the deck at my side and I was scratching his ears with one hand. Dina was beside me. I'd just talked to Heenan on the telephone. He said that my share of the money had been deposited in our bank account.

Dina reached out to grab my other hand.

"You know, this is one of the few times in life where everybody got what they wanted," she said. "Taft got Rosa back in prison, where he can squeeze information out of him from now until the end of time, plus the satisfaction of seeing Rosa's partnership with *La Puerca* blow up. Heenan got paid, which is mostly all he ever wants. Suarez got paid well, too, the equivalent of a free ride through law school. And Valencia was not only rein-stated, he was promoted."

I pointed out that part of the reason for the unex-pected promotion was no doubt due to the influence of, Valencia was shocked to learn, his father, General Urrea. It turned out that Valencia was Urrea's illegitimate son, only Valencia, now Captain Valencia, didn't know it.

"Don't mar the beauty of my analysis with your quib-bling little asides," she scolded. "I'm talking big picture here."

"Right," I agreed. "Big picture."

"There's another interesting little detail," I said. "Remember Rosa's girlfriend?"

Dina nodded.

"According to Heenan, Taft thinks that was *La Puerca* herself."

"Good God! Well at least that'll give Taft something to do."

"I'm sure he's got a lot to do, even if I still don't know who the hell he is or what he does," I said.

"It would be okay with me if you never saw that man again," she said.

"Me, too," I agreed. "But what about us, kid, what did we get out of this?"

"Each other," she said. "I think we came though this one even stronger than we were before."

"I like that," I said. "We wound up with a pot full of money, too."

"There's that," she said. "And you seemed to handle things pretty well, all things considered."

"There were some tough spots, but yeah, I think so," I said. "Call me crazy, but I may get along without a psychiatrist down here."

Dina squeezed my hand and gave me a fond look.

"Okay," she said, "you're crazy."

A LOOK AT: CABO
(CABO 2)

Private investigator mysteries don't usually come with palm trees, turquoise seas, and brutal kidnappings—but Ethan Cruickshank isn't your usual PI…

When four innocents are gunned down during a violent night raid in Cabo San Lucas, local police chief Valencia calls on a trusted friend—Ethan Cruickshank, the reluctant American detective still trying to leave the past behind. The target: the stunning young wife of a ruthless real estate mogul, snatched offshore by unknown assailants and vanished into the vast Baja wilderness.

What starts as a favor turns into a frantic manhunt as Ethan and Valencia chase a trail of riddles through a world where nothing is what it seems. From sun-drenched beaches to backwater desert outposts, they're joined by two sharp-edged American women whose shadowy pasts make them dangerous allies— and possibly more.

But as the case twists further from its clean-cut beginnings, Ethan is forced to ask himself: who really benefits from this abduction? And how many people have to die before the truth surfaces?

What you don't know really can kill you…

AVAILABLE AUGUST 2025

ABOUT THE AUTHOR

Robert Wisehart was born in Indianapolis, Indiana, and now is fortunate enough to live in Santa Fe, New Mexico.

In between Indianapolis and Santa Fe, he worked for many years as an award-winning reporter and columnist for newspapers in Florida, North Carolina, Louisiana and Northern and Southern California, plus occasional flirtations with radio and television as an on-air commentator. Such is the changing world that three of the four newspapers no longer exist.

Later, as a freelance writer, Wisehart did everything from write speeches to ghost books. He labored as a restaurant critic and for a brief time as a one of the dreaded horde of government consultants, two words that can mean almost anything but usually add up to not much. His work has appeared in more than 200 newspapers and 30 magazines, plus several digital outlets.

Wisehart and his wife, Dana, have been married for a lifetime and intend to make it a very long lifetime indeed. They have moved much, traveled well and Dana easily is the best thing that ever happened to him. Their two sons, Marc and Carl, live in New York City.